Liberty
Biscuit

Melanie Sue Bowles

Liberty
Biscuit

T
TRAFALGAR SQUARE
North Pomfret, Vermont

First published in 2022 by
Trafalgar Square Books
North Pomfret, Vermont 05053

The poem "Under the Sylvan Sun" by Lennon Faris appears by permission of the author.

Library of Congress Cataloging-in-Publication Data
Names: Bowles, Melanie Sue, 1957- author.
Title: Liberty Biscuit / Melanie Bowles.
Description: North Pomfret, Vermont : Trafalgar Square Books, 2022. |
  Summary: Thirteen-year-old Kip rescues a one-eyed white donkey and his
  two horse companions from an abusive owner, and, with the help of her
  Grandpa Joe, she works to gentle the hurt and frightened animals.
Identifiers: LCCN 2022011141 (print) | LCCN 2022011142 (ebook) | ISBN
  9781646011254 (paperback) | ISBN 9781646011261 (epub)
Subjects: CYAC: Donkeys--Fiction. | Horses--Fiction. | Families--Fiction. |
  Grief--Fiction. | Racially mixed people--Fiction. | Farm life--Fiction.
  | Georgia--Fiction. | LCGFT: Novels.
Classification: LCC PZ7.1.B68718 Li 2022 (print) | LCC PZ7.1.B68718
  (ebook) | DDC [Fic]--dc23
LC record available at https://lccn.loc.gov/2022011141
LC ebook record available at https://lccn.loc.gov/2022011142

Book design by *Katarzyna Misiukanis–Celińska (https://misiukanis-artstudio.com)*
Cover design by *RM Didier*
Typefaces: *Source Serif Pro* and *Playfair Display*

Printed in the United States of America

10 9 8 7 6 5 4 3 2 1

To Carolyn.

I wish you had seen the manuscript turn into a book.
We will love you and miss you forever.

acknowledgments

*H*undreds of animals have been welcomed to the pastures and paddocks at Proud Spirit Horse Sanctuary, which my husband Jim and I founded over thirty years ago. Some of their stories have broken our hearts, many have taught us valuable lessons in strength and perseverance as we navigated the disturbing world of rescue work, but all of them have given us immeasurable inspiration in one way or another.

The donkey portrayed in this book is based on a combination of two mischievous burros who arrived at the Sanctuary from different states, different neglectful situations. From the moment they were introduced, they bonded deeply and were inseparable for nearly twenty years. To Biscuit, thank you for the hilarious hijinks and endless shenanigans.

And dear Liberty, thank you for being his accomplice extraordinaire. We will never forget the joy and laughter, and a few incidents of momentary panic, you both brought to our lives.

A few years ago, I experienced soul-crushing racism. The hate wasn't directed at me, a white woman, but rather toward my white daughter who is with a Black man, and their children. The judgmental ignorance must end. This story was born out of a desire to normalize mixed-race families. Mixed-race families belong. To my granddaughters, Jeniyah and Janasia, you are smart and brave and strong. Beautiful inside and out. And you belong.

Thank you to the important people in my life who read a portion or an early version of the manuscript. My unfaltering champion, Jean McCormick; my dear brother, Mark Foster; my smart and savvy sister-in-law, Carolyn Foster; fellow author/friend, Casie Bazay; grammar afficionado/friend, Karen Sisson; writer/friend, Claire Bobrow. All of you believed this story had a powerful message, made suggestions for improvement, and encouraged me to keep going.

To award-winning author/friend, Jessica Keener: You are kind and gentle yet see the complicated intricacies of life with a fierce vision. The way you've always lifted me and my writing literally brings tears to my eyes.

Thank you to Lennon Faris for permission to use your fabulous poem "Under the Sylvan Sun."

I'd like to give a shout-out to three Annas (who don't even know each other):

Anna E. Nuckols, you have embraced a life of kindness, and you are making an impact on the people you touch.

Anna E. Ross, you are a bright light in a sometimes dark and scary world.

Anna M. Blake, you are changing the lives of horses and their humans. More importantly, you have created an enduring legacy of compassion for the future.

Thank you to everyone over at The Reef (Janet Reid!) and in The Writer's Room. The support we give each other is priceless, and I love you all.

Thank you Samantha Canup, DVM. We are beyond grateful for you and all you do.

To my husband Jim: You make everything possible. To our granddaughter Audrey Moon: We are so proud of who you are, of your outlook and the way you navigate life.

To the entire team at Trafalgar Square Books: I am profoundly grateful that Kip's story found a home with you. An especially huge thank you to editor Rebecca Didier. Your extraordinary professionalism made every chapter better. And because of you, the process of turning a messy manuscript into a book was actually fun.

prologue

*T*here are worse things than having an imaginary horse as your best friend. Like having no imagination at all, for instance. Which I imagine would be awful. I don't talk about horses to many people. Mostly just to Grandpa Joe.

Grandpa Joe says if you train a horse with kindness they'll walk with confidence and grace, and an animal as noble as a horse deserves to be confident. Stallions will swagger, geldings will strut, and mares will sashay. He should know. Every handed-down story reveals he was the finest horse trainer in all of Georgia, although it's not something he'd ever brag about. That was a long time ago, way before I was born.

Now, instead of horses, our family raises peaches. Acres and acres of peaches. But the memory of horses is in the air. Even if that memory isn't mine.

If you're wondering why I live on what used to be a horse farm but don't have one of my own, there's one great big unfortunate reason: Daddy won't allow anything equine that can still draw a breath anywhere on our property. In fact, Daddy won't allow pets at all. Any pet. Who ever heard of such a thing? It used to be an awful source of contention between us, but pleading with Daddy for a pet is the very definition of a lesson in futility. I quit asking.

You'd think the love of horses would be in Daddy's blood, as much as Grandpa Joe loves them and given the fact that Daddy was raised with them. But, nope. He won't talk about horses or even tell me why he doesn't like them. So the why of it remains a mystery. The how of it is a mystery, as well. As in, how can anyone dislike horses when there's so much about them to love? Maybe that particular gene skips a generation because I love horses more than anything in the world. Having one of my own is all I dream about.

Grandma Pearl used to say, "No dream ever came true without believing it would."

Trust me when I say I devoted myself to believing I'd have a horse one day. While I was waiting for that miracle to occur,

I conjured up an imaginary one. A mare. She has a sorrel coat that shimmers in the sun. Her forelock grows thick and long, clear down to the tip of her nose. Her flaxen mane dances in the wind and her tail touches the ground. She's tall and refined, and boy, does that mare sashay. She loves me as much as I love her. I imagined her so fully there were times I could smell her sweet earthy scent and see my own reflection in her liquid brown eyes. There were even times I thought I could hear her whinny echoing to me through the woods. That's how devoted I was to believing.

I also believe in magic. Not the kind with sorcerers wearing robes and pointy hats, casting spells and making brooms fly. No. What I believe in is more of a gentle magic.

The kind that turns the glow of the setting sun through the reds and yellows of autumn leaves into a carnival in the woods. Those same woods in the spring? It nearly takes my breath away when I come upon the snowflake white of a dogwood tree against the variegated greens of elms, oaks, and sweet gums unfurling new foliage. Or how, after a rain, the quartz rocks that protrude from the pine forest floor glisten and twinkle, and take on the appearance of a village for fairies.

All that? That's some gentle magic.

I'm convinced it was gentle magic that shaped the events of one hot morning in July. I was headed to my secret spot down by

Busby Creek, a meandering waterway that runs along the low side of our land. It's also a tributary of the Savannah River and therefore always flowing. The quickest way to get to the creek is a path through our two hundred acres of woods. But I was sticking to the red dirt lane because I was barefoot, and brambles and briars and pokey pinecones don't make for easy walking.

Although a better word to describe what I was doing might be *stomping*. I was somewhat angry over earlier events of the day. I was also carrying a sack of peach biscuits fresh from the oven.

I had just reached into the bag to eat one of those biscuits when I saw a sudden flash of movement in the woods. It was immediately followed by the four-beat thrum of hooves hitting the ground. I stopped so abruptly that the dust around my feet billowed on ahead of me. My eyes darted back and forth trying to catch sight of whatever it was. I could hear a whooshing sound and crunching leaves, snapping twigs and branches, and then...silence. Except for the pounding of my heart.

I knew it wasn't a deer. Deer are too stealthy. Deer are quiet. I'll admit right here and now, the idea that I'd finally dreamed my imaginary horse to life crossed my mind. I didn't dare move, afraid I'd disrupt the magic. Then, unbidden, the name I'd given her just came right out of my mouth. I spoke the words out loud. "Mary," I whispered, nearly breathless. "Is that you?"

I couldn't follow her into the woods because, as mentioned, I was barefoot. I now wished I had listened to Mama when she'd told me to put on a pair of shoes—there are times when my willfulness works to my advantage, and times when it does not.

More rustling came from the brush, then I heard another sharp snap of a twig. It sounded like whoever or whatever it was might be making their way to the creek. I broke into a run as I kept watch for any movement in the shadows of the dense brush. The sky was overcast and gray, the color of day-old oatmeal, but the light changed when I came to the end of the lane at Busby Creek, no longer under the canopy of trees. I approached the water and cautiously stepped onto the bank, then peered up and down the red clay shore.

Nothing.

I made some gentle kissing sounds. Then I whispered, "C'mon, girl. Where are you?" I stepped into the water to better see around a slight bend. I was wearing shorts and went in up to my knees. My back was to the woods.

Suddenly, a thunderous sound came crashing through the trees behind me. I gasped and reeled around; my eyes were as big and round as the O in holy. I held the bag of biscuits up like a shield, although what good I thought it would do to protect me from whatever was charging in my direction, I can't say. Could it really be my Mary?

There! A blur of white. My Mary wasn't white, but I felt breathless just the same. And then... then I heard the most awful screeching sound I've ever heard in my life. If I wasn't so shocked, I would've covered my ears.

"EEE EEE EEEEE-HAAAW!"

In a flurry of flailing pine boughs, a pure white donkey bound from the cover of overgrowth and came skidding to a stop not thirty feet from where I stood. I covered my mouth and held my breath. He looked slightly crazed as he took a few shuffling steps forward. It didn't appear he'd seen me.

I backed deeper into the water. The movement drew his attention. He swung his head till his eyes landed directly on mine. Well, I should say his *eye*, because he only had one. The left one. The right one was an empty hollow, which may be why he hadn't noticed me at first. With every bob of his head, his right ear drooped and lolled beside his cheek while the left one stood straight up. I noticed he was missing patches of hair over various sections of his body.

Clutching my bag of biscuits, I held my free hand up in the universal sign for stop, hoping he wouldn't come any closer.

"Whoa, there, little fella," I said. I relaxed a bit and dropped my shoulders.

He responded to the sound of my voice with another screeching bray.

"EEE EEE EEEEE-HAAAW!"

I just stood there, blinking rapidly as though I'd been unkindly slapped across the face. "Good grief," I said out loud. If you could get past the sheer volume of his bray, it might have been described as a jovial sound.

Now we were staring at each other. I couldn't decide if he was going to charge like a billy goat and knock me down or turn and flee back through the woods. I took a few steps sideways. He mimicked me and took a few gangly steps closer. The knee of his right leg was terribly crooked and he walked with a limp. We continued to stare at each other. Now I was afraid to blink. Finally, the donkey nodded, just once. Or maybe he was trying to displace a fly. But I nodded back. Then I smiled at him. He appeared to smile back.

"You look hungry," I said. I reached into the bag and withdrew a biscuit. "Are you hungry? Here."

Still wary—I didn't want to get knocked down, kicked, or bitten—I stretched my arm in his direction and offered him the goods. His nostrils began to twitch like the beating wings of a hummingbird. Without warning, he leaped into the water where I was standing, splashing me. I was momentarily startled and shuffled backwards, but he gently popped his lips against the food in my hand until he'd devoured the entire thing. Minnows gathered around our legs to nibble the crumbs that had fallen into the water.

Upon the final swallow, the donkey opened and closed his mouth a few times as though he were trying to determine exactly what it was he'd just eaten.

"You're in no position to be fussy," I told him. "You're teetering on skin-and-bones." He apparently decided peach biscuits tasted just fine as he commenced to swindle me out of another one by tipping his head sideways and batting his left eye in a most adorable way. I was now quite certain he was not a danger.

"Where'd you come from, fella?" I asked while he ate another biscuit. He didn't answer. "You sure are a scruffy-looking thing." I moved out of the water and stepped up the bank. The donkey followed, licking my hand to get the last of the buttery crumbs. I reached for a third one. "Did you run away from home? I don't recollect anyone around here keeping donkeys. Or did some mean old soul dump you out here?"

He finished the third biscuit, then looked at me, expectantly, batting his one good eye.

"That's enough for now," I told him. "We need to figure out what to do with you."

I stuffed the bag with the remaining biscuits down the front of my shirt to free my hands, then stepped carefully into the woods, avoiding thorns and pinecones. I found what I was looking for: wild wisteria. I pulled out my pocket knife—no self-respecting farm girl from Georgia goes anywhere without her pocket knife—and cut about twenty feet of the tough but pliable vine. I braided the vine back on itself, then made a loop and a band, fashioning it into a halter of sorts with about four feet remaining to act as a lead. The donkey accepted it unflinchingly as I slipped it over his head. We started walking home. The halter proved unnecessary as the pitiful little creature kept his nose pressed against my hip.

Glancing back at him, I felt a heavy sadness over the sorry condition he was in. I sighed deeply as I gave his scrawny neck a gentle scratch, and then I laughed. At myself. So much for dreams coming true. It figures I'd wind up with a bedraggled broken-down donkey rather than my glorious Mary. Just more of my quirky luck, I thought, and laughed again.

But somehow, fate was rigged in my favor... I just didn't know it at the time. And it all began with that sack of biscuits.

chapter 1

" Katherine Pearl!" Mama called through the open kitchen window. That's me. Katherine Pearl Baker. Katherine after my mama's mother, who I call Grandma Kay. Grandma Kay and Grandpa Earl live up north, outside of Detroit on a freshwater lake. That's where Mama was born and raised. The Pearl part of my name is after my daddy's mother, who I call Grandma Pearl. At least that's what I used to call her. Grandma Pearl passed away a little over a year ago, and nothing around here has ever been the same. Especially Grandpa Joe. He misses her terribly. We all do. But it's as if Grandma Pearl took a part of Grandpa Joe with her when she left this earth.

Mama is the only one who calls me Katherine Pearl. Everyone else calls me Kip. Some of my friends say it's a clear indication they're in trouble when their mama uses both their first and middle names. Not me. Mama uses both my names purely for the way the delightful sound rolls off her tongue—those are her words.

I was sitting on the steps of our back porch reading a book when Mama called to me. I read a lot. I read a lot of books featuring horses. Books and horses are two of my favorite things. And words. I love words. Porches in the South are actually called verandas. That's a great word: *veranda*. Ours is wide and wraps around the entire house. The back side provides a good view of the woods and a decent escape from the steamy Georgia sun.

The woods are an even better escape. I swear, the air feels ten degrees cooler in the woods. It's like another world. I have a secret place I like to go down by Busby Creek. A thick stand of sweet gums grows right beside the water, and there's a mysterious outcropping of moss-covered rocks and boulders in the center of those trees. Some of the boulders are the size of a Volkswagen Beetle. When there's a breeze, even a calm one, it causes the water to lap the shore and coaxes the leaves into a pleasant vibration above my head. I sit hidden among the rocks and close my eyes, listening and breathing, and it takes no effort at all for my mind to clear. If you were to ask me for one word to describe this place, that word would be *enchanted*.

"Yes, Mama?" I answered as I closed my book and got up from the steps. I'd been listening to Mama as she bustled back and forth in the kitchen. I could also smell a batch of peach biscuits, fresh from the oven. We eat a lot of peaches around here, prepared in a vast variety of ways, even grilled.

My daddy farms four hundred acres of orchards. Baker Peach Farm, Inc. *One Bite and You'll Have a Peach of a Day!* Grandma Pearl came up with that slogan nearly fifty years ago, back when she and Grandpa Joe first bought this farm. They started with just fifty acres and a little three-room clapboard cottage. Back then, Grandpa Joe was raising and training horses. He built a sturdy post-and-beam barn with his own two hands. It was four times the size of the house, which is gone now. The house, I mean. That big beautiful barn is still standing.

As much as Grandpa Joe loved horses, they weren't bringing in much of a living. So Grandpa Joe and Grandma Pearl got into peaches. Over the years they bought more and more land, and planted more and more trees. That meant fewer and fewer horses, until there were none. They eventually built a bigger house, away from the barn. It's the house we all live in now. My daddy was raised here. He always worked the farm, even as a child.

Mama moved here to the farm after she and Daddy got married. They met when Mama had come south to get away from the cold Michigan winters and attend college in Savannah. Daddy was there taking some business classes. Daddy says he worked harder at turning Mama's head than he did in an entire year on the farm. He says she was the smartest, prettiest girl he'd ever laid eyes on and he never believed for one second she'd ever fall for a farm boy from Georgia. Mama laughs like a young girl when Daddy talks this way.

"Charles J. Baker," she always says, "you had me at 'hello.'"

I love hearing about the days when they were dating.

I was born a few years after they were married. Just me. Just like Daddy, I'm an only child. When I was younger, I hoped for a brother or a sister. I even asked Mama if we were going to have more kids. She just smiled and said, "Heck, no! We created perfection on the first try." But a look of sadness shadowed her face, so I never asked her again.

Our house sits at the south edge of those rows and rows of fruit trees, all lined up like soldiers. The back porch, as mentioned, overlooks the woods. Thankfully. I prefer the tangle of nature to the order of human intervention.

I got up and went in the house.

"Yes, Mama?" I repeated as I walked into the kitchen.

"Katherine Pearl, I need you to take some food up to your daddy," Mama said as she plucked steaming biscuits off a hot baking sheet with an oven mitt and stuffed them into a paper sack. The melting butter seeped through the brown paper, making dark shiny circles. "He's in the equipment barn. One of the tractors isn't running. He can't stop for lunch, but he needs something to eat." She pushed the bag across the center island, then went to the sink. "Go on, now," she said without looking at me. She put the plug in the drain, turned the water on, and then added a squirt of dish soap.

"But what about the parade?" I asked over the sound of the running water.

"See if Grandpa Joe wants one," Mama said over her shoulder, not answering my question. "He's working in the garden."

"Mama," I said, speaking louder, "what about the parade? It's the Fourth of July."

The baking sheet, several mixing bowls, and a handful of utensils clattered in the sink as Mama began washing them. I saw her lift one shoulder and shake her head.

"I can't leave the farm today, Katherine. I've got clients coming."

"On a holiday? Geez, Mama."

Mama is a CPA. Certified Public Accountant. She's brilliant with numbers. Me? I prefer words over numbers. I guess math skills are something else that skipped a generation, along with the love of horses. Mama used to have an office in town, but after Grandma Pearl died, she set up an office here at the farm and parted with quite a few of her clients. She apparently thought I was spending too much time alone. For all the good it did. I still spend most of my time alone.

"Well, it couldn't be helped," Mama replied. "Anyway, it's your Uncle Dale and Aunt Betty. Today's the only day both of them could go over their finances at the same time. They're gonna stay for our cookout later this afternoon." She glanced in my direction—trying to read the expression on my face, I suspected—then she turned back to the sink, adding, "Aunt Betty's making a red velvet cake."

"That's nice," I muttered. Dale and Betty Miller aren't really my aunt and uncle. They're Mama and Daddy's closest friends. And our closest neighbors. If I cut through the woods and walk fast, I can make it to their house in a half-hour.

They don't have kids, but they do have two horses. Fancy, a dark bay Arabian mare, and Prism, a Paint gelding. That right there is worth the walk. I'd gladly do it every day for the opportunity to brush those horses and help with the chores. Aunt Betty takes me trail riding now and then. I usually ride Prism. But Aunt Betty and Uncle Dale are as busy as Mama and Daddy, so I don't get to go over there very often.

"Go on, now," Mama said again as she tipped her head in the direction of the equipment barn. Then she added, "And put some shoes on. You can't go up there with bare feet."

I wondered how she knew I wasn't wearing any shoes. She'd hardly looked at me. I stood for a moment, staring at her back. I forgot to be angry as I admired the way Mama had used a narrow scarf to hold her hair up and keep it off her face. She'd tied the ends on top of her head and they flopped to the side like bunny ears. It gave her a youthful appearance. The scarf was one I was particularly fond of, with its bright colors and interesting paisley design. Mama sure had a certain flair about her. A simple elegance. That's something not easily achieved on a peach farm in the middle of nowhere. I wondered if I'd ever be as pretty as her.

Finally, recalling the task at hand, I sighed dramatically and dragged the sack of biscuits off the island, then headed for the door.

"Katherine Pearl," Mama said, stopping me. "What's the word of the day?"

"We don't have one," I answered glumly.

Mama and I have a game we play where we flip through the dictionary till we come upon a word I'm unfamiliar with or one that has an unusual sound or meaning. We use the word in as many ways as we can throughout the day. We don't play the game every day, but one of our most recent words was *festooned*. Mama made a peach pie *festooned* with raspberries. Daddy's ball cap *festooned* his head. We try to make each other laugh.

"How about *grateful* as the word of the day?" Mama said as she continued to wash the dishes.

"That's not unusual," I said.

"No?" Mama said. "Seems to me that being grateful is a rare and unusual thing around this farm today."

Now I saw what Mama was doing. In a roundabout way she was scolding me for my lousy attitude. "It's just that—" I began.

"Let me use it in a sentence," Mama interrupted. "When we walk a path of ungratefulness, we make the journey long, lonely, and difficult."

"I thought the word was grateful," I said in a sassy tone of voice, clearly pushing my luck, but I couldn't seem to stop myself.

Mama turned and gave me the stink eye. That's when one eyebrow is arched high and the other one is set in a scowl. I always marveled over the skill this required. A skill I did not possess. I'd even practiced in the mirror. I only succeeded in looking like I'd just inhaled a moth.

"Go," Mama said pointing in the direction of the equipment barn while soap bubbles dripped from her finger. "And put some shoes on!"

In the two seconds it took for me to get from the kitchen to the back door I conveniently forgot about the shoes. I hated wearing shoes. That's another thing Mama scolds me for, saying the word hate. She prefers the word dislike. She says hate is a powerful emotion and you shouldn't go through life hating much in this great big marvelous world. But I'm here to tell you I hate shoes.

Hurrying past the kitchen window so Mama wouldn't see me and my bare feet, I went to find Grandpa Joe. He was bent over a cucumber vine, searching for ones ready to be picked. The love of gardening was another thing we shared, besides horses. We spent a lot of time out here together. And we solved a lot of problems. You'd be surprised how easy it is to work through a despondency in your heart when your hands are busy in the dirt.

"Hey, Kipper," he said when he saw me. A little smile tugged at the corners of his mouth, but it never reached his eyes. The fact that he called me Kipper, though, was cause for a bit of cheer in my heart. That's what he always used to call me, before Grandma Pearl died.

"Mama made peach biscuits," I told him, smiling and holding the bag aloft as a visual aid. "Want one? Or two?"

"None." Grandpa Joe shook his head as he lifted both hands, palm side up to display the dirt from the garden. "I'll have some later," he said.

"Wanna walk up to the equipment barn with me? One of the tractors is broke down and Daddy needs something to eat." I gave his sleeve a tug and lifted the bag again for emphasis.

"Not right now, Kip." He patted my hand and turned back to the cucumbers.

"I bet you'd know how to fix the tractor. Then we could go to the parade."

"What parade?" Grandpa asked.

My eyes popped open in disbelief. "Grandpa! It's the Fourth of July. The parade. In town. Am I the only person on this farm who cares that it's the Fourth of July?"

"A farm doesn't care about what day it is, Kip. You know that. Running a farm doesn't take a holiday."

"Which is precisely why I'm *not* gonna be a farmer," I said.

Grandpa Joe didn't respond. He just kept searching through the scratchy cucumber vines while I stared at his back, willing him to turn around and give me a real smile, then announce that he and I would go to town, just the two of us, to watch the parade.

"Grandpa," I finally said. "What about the horses?"

"What about them, Kip?"

"You love seeing the horses." Then I added, "And we missed the parade last year." The very second those words left my mouth I wanted to suck them right back in. We missed the parade last year because Grandma Pearl had just died. Now my cheeks were burning and I felt like the biggest idiot on earth. Grandpa Joe's hands got still and from where I stood it looked like someone let the air out of his lungs. "Maybe next year," he said quietly. "Better get that food up to your daddy." I tried not to let my eyes fill with tears. Not that it mattered. Who would see? Nobody, that's who. I took a few steps backward, then turned and ran all the way to the barn where Daddy was working. But it wasn't a happy run, it was an angry one. Angry at myself for making Mama mad and making Grandpa Joe feel sadder than he already did.

The bay doors of the barn were wide open and I could hear the tractor running. I stood outside for a minute to catch my breath and dry my eyes. Daddy didn't see me till I stepped into his line of sight. He offered a quick wave.

"Mama made peach biscuits," I hollered over the roar of the diesel engine and, once again, held the bag aloft.

"Not now, honey." Daddy shook his head, and just as Grandpa Joe had done, he lifted his hands, palms up. I could see they were covered in grease. I set the bag on his workbench and stood beside him.

"Is the tractor fixed?" I asked, glad to hear it running.

"Nope," he said. "Still not running right. Hear that high-pitched whistle sound?"

I nodded.

"I can't get the RPMs up. PTO won't run."

I nodded again, understanding. You might think a girl of thirteen years old wouldn't know what all that meant, but I did. RPMs stands for *revolutions per minute*. That's how many turns the engine takes in one minute. And PTO stands for *power train operation*. The power train is what runs the implements that attach to the tractor, things like the bucket and the mower. If the engine isn't running fast enough, you can't operate the attachments.

"Daddy," I said. "Are we gonna make it to town for the Fourth of July parade?"

"Afraid not, Kip." He wiped his face with a rag. "Mama's got clients coming."

"She told me. But I thought you and I—"

"I have to get this tractor running. We got harvest soon. Did you ask Grandpa if he wanted to go? Maybe the two of you..." Daddy's voice trailed off as he focused his attention on the tractor.

I shifted my eyes down to the ground and shook my head. Once again, shame burned my cheeks over bringing up missing the parade last year. Thankfully, Daddy didn't notice. He was facing away from me. I stared at his back. Seemed like I was spending a lot of time staring at people's backs.

"I'll see ya later," I said and started toward the door.

"Kip," Daddy called. I turned around, hopeful he had changed his mind about going to town. But he just pointed at the bag of biscuits on his workbench. "Don't leave those. I'll forget about 'em and they'll draw ants."

I huffed out another exasperated sigh as I snatched the bag off the workbench. I could feel another round of anger rising in my chest. But this time it was directed at my family, rather than myself. I ran out of the barn where Daddy was busy with the tractor. I ran past Mama busy in the house. I ran past Grandpa Joe busy in the garden. I didn't slow down till I came to the dirt lane that cuts through the middle of our woods. Time in the woods would tamp down my anger. It always did. I slowed my run to a deliberate stomp, then settled into a walk as I headed for Busby Creek, taking several deep breaths as I went.

It crossed my mind to wander over to the old Homestead where Grandpa Joe and Grandma Pearl lived when they were first married. But then I thought about that beautiful horse barn, neglected now and overgrown with brambles. The falling-down fences, the tipped-over water troughs, and the empty paddocks—the empty paddocks were the worst part—only served to make me sad.

I needed to forget about the fact that everybody was too busy for me and too busy for the fun in town. The whole world could just go on and celebrate the Fourth of July without the Baker family.

Well, I guess the celebrations would be limited to the good ol' United States of America, but you get my drift. At least we were going to have a cookout with Uncle Dale and Aunt Betty.

As I walked toward the creek, I paused when I came to Flat Rock, a large rock on the edge of the road that seems to have randomly popped up out of nowhere. Flat Rock was about the size of an extra-large coffee table, and just as flat as one, too. That's why I named him Flat Rock. I almost named him Lonely Rock, but then I came to the realization that I didn't actually know if this rock was lonely. Why saddle him with my perceptions?

The reason I paused at Flat Rock was because I'd recently read about a girl in Japan who befriended a flock of crows. She left food for them in the same spot every day, and then she would call to them as she walked away using a few code words, always in the same tone of voice. In turn, the crows eventually began leaving her gifts—bits of string, bottle caps, broken glass—in the same spot she left their food.

Spurred by Daddy's dismal no-pet policy and inspired by the Japanese girl's astonishing success, I decided having a flock of crows as friends might be pretty darn terrific. Did you know that a flock of crows is actually called...a murder?

Like a herd of horses or a school of fish or a gaggle of geese. A murder of crows. Isn't that a strange and interesting fact?

I'm just fascinated with the names given to groups of animals. They're called "collective nouns." One of my favorites is a *dazzle of zebras*. I love that!

I'd been leaving food on Flat Rock in an attempt to befriend the crows in our woods for nearly a month. The article about the girl in Japan didn't reveal what code words she used, but I decided to try speaking to them in their own language and had settled on the words, "Caw! Caw!" I'm not sure how this translated to the crows. I hoped I was saying something along the lines of, "Hello! Here's some food and I hope we can be friends and if you'd like to bring me gifts that would be spectacular but is not a requirement." So far, they hadn't brought me any gifts, but I wasn't ready to give up.

I pulled out one of the peach biscuits I was carrying and crumbled it across Flat Rock. I searched the treetops for a moment, then backed away, calling, "Caw! Caw!"

I continued on toward Busby Creek and decided to eat one of the biscuits myself. That's when I caught a glimpse of the apparition out of the corner of my eye.

chapter 2

*T*hat apparition turned out to be this raggedy little donkey who insisted on keeping some part of his body touching mine. It was as though he thought I might disappear if we were separated and he wasn't going to risk it.

As odd as it may sound, I'd already developed quite an affection for him. Our time together amounted to under two hours, but I felt we were tethered to each other by more than the braided wisteria vine. He seemed to need me, and I'll admit, I liked the way being needed felt.

The donkey and I stood at the edge of the woods, staring at the house, while a flutter of butterflies knocked around in my stomach. I'd spent the long walk home trying to think of a way to sell Daddy on the idea of finally letting me have a pet.

I suppose someone smarter than me would've taken another stab at this old argument with, say, a hamster or a lizard. Not me. I had the audacity to launch my attack with a three-hundred-pound donkey who looked like he'd been through the wringer. Go big or go home.

There wasn't any movement from behind the wide row of windows in our kitchen. I wondered if Mama was in her office. Grandpa Joe must've finished working in the garden and gone inside. I shifted my eyes up the gravel drive toward the equipment barn. The bay doors were closed. That meant Daddy had finished working and was probably in the house getting cleaned up for company and our cookout.

I draped my arm over the donkey's back. "I don't know how it happened, in so short a time, but I sure do love you." I spoke the words quietly. "And I sure do wanna keep you." The donkey shuffled forward and pressed his cheek against my hip. "Now, listen to me...we're gonna face some fierce opposition." I leaned down to look into his good eye. "You hear me? But if you behave yourself and act like a gentleman, we just might have a shot at this. In other words, just stand there, quiet-like."

Truth be told, I doubted we actually did "have a shot," but the moment called for a positive outlook. The donkey looked back at me and blinked his one eye several times. "Daddy's not a bad sort," I continued. "In fact, in all ways I'd say he's the best daddy in the world. He's A+ across the board. Except when it comes to keeping pets. And anything to do with horses. Then he gets a D-."

The donkey gave me a nudge.

"I know. You're not a horse. But you're in the equine family and Daddy will regard you as a nuisance, just the same."

Looking back at the house, I took a very deep breath and held it as long as I could. As I let it out, I whispered, "It's now or never..."

"What in the world!" Mama's face suddenly appeared in the kitchen window.

I smiled and wiggle-waggled my fingers in a casual wave as though a donkey attached to my hip were an everyday occurrence.

"Oh, Kip," she said through the open window. Except the words came out more like a groan. Her brow was furrowed. "Where did you find a donkey?"

Before I could answer, Mama turned and walked briskly toward the back door. "The poor thing looks like he's starving," she said when she joined us in the backyard.

"He is starving, Mama." My tone of voice was urgent. "I found him in the woods." I looked at her with pleading eyes and added, "He needs me."

Mama reached out to run a hand down the donkey's neck. He turned to smell her arm. Then he licked her. Mama and I both couldn't help but chuckle. He must have realized she was the source of those peach biscuits.

"Isn't he the sweetest thing, Mama? I just love him. Couldn't we keep him?"

"Oh, Kip. If it was just up to me...but I don't know what Daddy will say."

Mama hadn't seemed to agree with Daddy's no-pet policy over the years, but it was also a topic she backed away from. She never tried to change his mind. I always wondered why.

"Daddy says he'll be calling the sheriff to come get some stray livestock off his property."

Mama and I quickly turned to see Daddy standing on the porch. His hands were stuck on his hips and his eyes were fixed in an unpleasant stare. I found it curious that he was speaking in the third person. I considered doing the same. *Kip found this donkey in the woods and she'd like to keep him. She thinks he's precious.* But then I quickly decided it wouldn't be the wisest way to win Daddy's heart.

"Daddy," I began. Mama put her hand on my arm, quieting me.

"Charles, just wait a minute," she said.

"Wait for what, Elise?" Daddy dropped his hands to his sides and came down the steps.

"Daddy, please," I said. Mama gripped my arm and gave me a gentle shake, once again silently asking me to be quiet.

"*Wait*, Charles, to make a decision until we've discussed this like a family," Mama said crossing her own arms over her chest in a show of conviction. I was surprised, but proud she was standing up for me.

"Discussed this!" Daddy said as his eyebrows shot nearly up into his hairline. "There's nothing to discuss. This animal either belongs to someone or he's been abandoned. Either way, he's not staying here."

I had hoped my positive outlook would create a favorable outcome. I knew Daddy wouldn't be pleased, but I thought there might be a blink of consideration. A blip. I would have taken a blip.

"Well, if he belongs to someone," Mama said, "they haven't taken very good care of him."

"He may have been missing for weeks," Daddy coldly reasoned. "Or longer, by the looks of him."

"I agree we should call the sheriff to see if someone has reported him missing. But if he is homeless, or he comes from a home where he was neglected, I think we should talk about allowing Katherine to keep him." Now Mama stuck her hands on her hips.

"I would like to keep him, Daddy," I said.

Daddy was already shaking his head. "You know how I feel about pets."

"Look how good he is," I said, trying not to sound like I was whining. "He won't be any trouble, Daddy."

"The expense," Daddy said.

"He can graze the orchards," said Mama. "We have hundreds of acres of free food."

"He needs to be seen by a vet. He looks half-dead and wormy. And he needs his hooves trimmed. All of that costs money."

"I'll bet Grandpa Joe will know what to do," I said. "We don't need a vet. Grandpa Joe knows everything about horses. And he can teach me to trim his hooves."

"Donkeys are nothing but trouble. Mischief. And what about the mess? The manure?"

"I'll watch over him, and I'll clean up after him. I promise."

Suddenly, as though he'd just been standing around waiting for the perfect opportunity, the donkey lifted his tail and made an awful grunting sound. Then manure plopped to the ground near Daddy's feet. I bit my lip and turned my face away to hide my smile. Mama put her hand over her mouth while her shoulders shook with muffled laughter.

Then Mama exclaimed, "Fertilizer! For the garden." There was a touch of awe in her voice as though the donkey had performed a magic trick. And then she reached for Daddy's hand. "He really is very sweet, Charles."

Just then, the donkey swung around, pointed his backside directly at Daddy, and lifted one hoof in an agitated way.

"Sweet?" Daddy said, backing away.

I tugged on the makeshift lead rope to move the donkey forward so he had to put his foot down. "You're not making this any easier," I growled in his good ear.

"He can sense you don't like him," Mama told Daddy.

"And he'd be right," Daddy said. "If he doesn't have a home, Sheriff Ronnie can take him to auction."

I gasped. "Daddy, no! The auction is a horrible place. All the animals are so scared." I wrapped my arms around the donkey's head. He shut his eyes and leaned against me. "He'd just end up going to slaughter. Please, Daddy."

One day last summer, Grandpa Joe and I had stopped at the livestock auction. He wanted to look at the horses. But we both became upset over the way the animals were treated and how the horses were all so nervous and skinny. We overheard a man say that most of them would "go to slaughter."

I remember feeling sick. Grandpa Joe said it hadn't been like that when he was a young man and involved in the horse world. He blamed overbreeding and irresponsible people who didn't make a commitment to their animals. He grumbled about it the entire ride back home. We both said we'd never go back.

"Listen to me, Kip—" Daddy began.

Suddenly, the donkey lifted his head in a most dramatic way and drew himself up to his full height, such as it was. He stomped a front hoof, just once, while taking a deep breath. Then he let out a mighty and agonized bray. It was even louder than when he'd come crashing out of the woods earlier.

"EEE, EEE, EEEEE-HAAAW!" And then he did it again. And again. And again.

And then, at the very moment the donkey finished trumpeting his final syllable, Mama, Daddy, and I were all shocked to hear another sound. A sound we hadn't heard in a long time. And it was coming from the porch.

Grandpa Joe was laughing.

chapter 3

"I just got off the phone with Ronnie," Daddy said. Ronnie was Sheriff Ronnie Alton. He and Daddy'd gone to school together and known each other their whole lives. When Daddy went in the house to call him, Grandpa Joe and I'd found an old bucket and filled it with water for the donkey. We'd put it in the shade of a willow tree. I'd removed the wisteria vine halter, then the donkey moved off to graze in the yard while keeping me in his line of sight.

"Any reports of a missing donkey?" Grandpa Joe asked.

Daddy shook his head. "Nope. But, believe it or not, just a few days ago Ronnie seized two starving horses from an abusive home, along with a white donkey."

"Oh, no," Mama said. "So he was being neglected. Along with two horses?"

Daddy nodded. "Looks that way. Ronnie and one of his deputies transported all three of them to the fairgrounds. As they were unloading them," Daddy paused and tipped his head at the donkey, "this rascal got loose and bolted. They've been looking for him for three days."

"The fairgrounds are over ten miles away," Grandpa said.

"Ronnie suspects he ran to the river, drawn by the smell of the water, then followed the shore till he ended up in our woods."

No, I thought. *He was searching for me.* I felt a wave of something difficult to describe come over me. The only reason I'd been in the woods earlier was because I'd been mad. But I saw now the events of this day had played out exactly as they were supposed to.

"If we had gone into town to see the parade," I said out loud, "he and I might never have found each other." Tears welled up in my eyes. I considered Mama's earlier word of the day: *grateful.* I surely was. What seemed like one of the lousiest days of my life had turned into one of the best.

"Keeping him hasn't been settled, Kip," Daddy said. "Also, Sheriff Ronnie is on his way over here. He needs to make certain this is in fact the same donkey he just confiscated." Daddy glanced over at Mama and shrugged. But then he turned his eyes to Grandpa Joe, who was shadowing the donkey as he grazed. Grandpa Joe was smiling and gently petting him. I saw Daddy's face soften.

"Charles, please," Mama said as she slipped her soft, slender hand into Daddy's rough and calloused one. Mama tilted her head and their eyes met. Daddy shrugged again and smiled, and gave her a tiny nod I almost didn't see.

I nearly fell to my knees with joy.

"That's him, all right," Sheriff Ronnie said. He hitched his thumbs in his gun belt, making the leather squeak and groan. His face was shaded from the sun by the white straw cowboy hat he wore as part of his uniform. I thought he was a handsome man and often wondered if I had a crush on him. "What happens now?" Mama asked.

"Well, this goes to court where the judge will decide whether or not all three animals will be returned to the owner."

"Returned!" I cried.

Sheriff Ronnie looked at me with a kind sympathy. "It happens all the time, Kip. And I hate it, believe me. But the laws don't always work in the favor of livestock."

"What will happen in the meantime, Ronnie?" Daddy asked. "Before this goes to court, I mean. Who takes care of the animals?"

Sheriff Ronnie removed his hat and pushed his hair off his forehead, then looked from Mama to Daddy. "I was going to talk to you about that," he said. "Aside from being thin, the horses appear sickly. We've had Doc Sam out."

Doc Sam was Dr. Samantha Caldwell, our local veterinarian. Not that I'd ever had any use for her services, as I didn't enjoy the companionship of a pet, but I knew her name from around town.

"She's tending to them," Sheriff Ronnie continued, "but they need to be quarantined till we get some bloodwork back. They're fine at the fairgrounds for now. And normally that's where confiscated livestock stays. But there's a horse show coming up. I need to move them, in case they're contagious, before horses begin arriving from all over the state."

My ears perked up over the direction this conversation appeared to be heading. I turned quick-like to look at Grandpa. Our eyes met and I was certain his were sparkling. He stopped petting the donkey and moved closer to where we all were standing.

Then Sheriff Ronnie said the magic words. "I wanted to ask if you'd help me out and let them come here?"

Daddy frowned. "What about Dale and Betty?" he suggested. "They're horse people."

"Quarantine, Charlie. I need to quarantine them. Dale and Betty have horses. Putting them with other horses isn't in quarantine. Your place is perfect for horses."

Right then and there, I decided what I had was indeed a crush on this lawman. I didn't want to ever forget the most beautiful words ever spoken: *Your place...is perfect for horses.*

"We aren't set up for livestock," Daddy said, still shaking his head in opposition. "We got no place to put them."

"Yes, we do," interjected Grandpa Joe. Everyone turned. "We can put them over at the Homestead."

Daddy sighed. "Have you been over there lately? The fences are falling down. Daddy, you can't even open the barn doors for all the overgrown weeds. And what about water? The well-pump has probably been seized up for ten years."

Grandpa Joe stuck his hands in the front pockets of his jeans and stared at Daddy. "You have no idea how often I go over there, son," he said. I thought I saw his chin quivering and it scared me. I had never seen Grandpa Joe cry; I knew he'd cried over Grandma Pearl, but not in front of me. Then Grandpa took a deep breath and narrowed his eyes. "And the last time I checked, I believe my name is on the deed of that particular fifty acres."

"Yes, sir," was all Daddy said.

"I also believe it's about time you get over this foolish objection you have to horses."

Daddy swallowed hard. He twisted his mouth to the side. "Yes, Daddy."

I looked over at Mama, unsure about what was happening. I had never heard Daddy sound like a child being scolded. And I don't mean the fact that he called Grandpa "Daddy." Farm boys from Georgia call their fathers "Daddy" even after they become grown men. It's just the way it is in the South. But Grandpa Joe and Daddy speaking to each other like a father scolding a child? It made my head feel light and my stomach feel queasy.

Mama gave me a slight nod and mouthed the words, "It's okay." The calm look on her face assured me everything was fine, or it would be, eventually. Her expression also seemed to say she agreed with Grandpa Joe.

Grandpa Joe turned to the sheriff. "Ronnie, if you'll give me and Kip three or four days to get the barn and at least one paddock cleaned up, you can move the horses to the Homestead." Then Grandpa looked at me. "Kip?" he said. "You on board with this plan?"

Before I could answer, Sheriff Ronnie lifted his hands in surrender and said, "I don't want to cause problems. But if you all agree..."

I looked at Daddy, not wishing to ignore his authority.

Daddy nodded.

I turned to Grandpa, unable to contain my smile. "Yes, sir," I said. But it came out as a breathless whisper. I didn't even know if he'd heard me. "Yes, sir!" I said again, louder. "I am *so* on board."

Grandpa said, "It's settled then."

"I sure appreciate this," Sheriff Ronnie said. "Just don't forget, the long-term fate of these horses is up in the air till we hear from Judge Andrews." He looked at me and pointed a finger. "Don't get attached." He added that he'd be in touch and bade us all good day.

Grandpa walked over to Daddy and clapped him on the shoulder. Then he said something only Daddy could hear. I thought it sounded like, *it's time to let it go, son*, but I couldn't be sure. Daddy turned to go back in the house. Mama went after him. I watched them walk away.

I felt mixed-up about everything that had just happened. Questions milled around in my head. One part of my brain knew Daddy was Grandpa Joe's son. I'd just never thought of Daddy as a child.

But then Grandpa Joe called my name and all that pondering got pushed to the side.

"Kipper!" he called in a happy tone of voice. I ran to him and threw myself into his arms. Grandpa Joe held me while my tears of joy speckled his shirt. When he gently pulled away

I could see tears in his eyes. I wondered if they were for the same reason as mine. We smiled at each other. Then Grandpa ruffled my hair and said, "We need to name this donkey. How about Liberty, for the Fourth of July?"

"I was thinking Biscuit."

We both laughed, and then, at the exact same time said, "Liberty Biscuit!"

Later that afternoon, Aunt Betty and Uncle Dale arrived. They spent over an hour in Mama's office going over their taxes while Daddy, Grandpa Joe, and I went about setting up the back patio for the cookout.

I had insisted everyone wear red, white, and blue in honor of the holiday. I was wearing a sleeveless blue cotton blouse with white stars, blue shorts, and a red bandana around my neck. Daddy was wearing blue slacks, a white tee-shirt, and a red ball cap. Grandpa was wearing blue jean shorts and a red-and-white-striped button-down shirt.

Mama had set out a blue tablecloth before heading to her office with Uncle Dale and Aunt Betty. Grandpa helped me spread it smoothly on the picnic table.

Daddy carried a cooler out. I could hear the ice and canned drinks sloshing around inside. He set it beside the table, then frowned as he looked at Grandpa.

"Your knee is swollen more than usual, Daddy," he said.

Grandpa sat down. "I know, son," he said rubbing his bad knee. "I'm getting closer and closer to going forward with that knee replacement."

"I wish you'd do it, Grandpa," I said. "It makes me hurt to see you hurting."

"I know, Kipper. Maybe this fall."

When Mama, Aunt Betty, and Uncle Dale joined us in the backyard, I introduced Liberty Biscuit. He happily grazed while I had a difficult time taking my eyes off him. I couldn't believe he was standing in my yard.

Aunt Betty exclaimed at his poor condition, but said she felt certain he'd be on the mend in no time at all. "Your Grandpa Joe will help you get him healthy and back on his feet," she assured me as she put her arm around my shoulder.

Uncle Dale stared at Liberty with his forehead crinkled in concern. "Hey, Charlie," he said. "Did Ronnie tell you the name of the person who owned him?"

Daddy shook his head. "Why?" he asked.

"About a year ago, maybe more," Uncle Dale began, but then he paused and looked over at me as if he wasn't sure he should continue. "Um...do you know Len Parker?"

Daddy said he didn't.

"No matter. About a year ago, one day at the feed store, I overheard Len Parker talking about a white donkey he'd just brought home. He said his white color was rare. He was laughing about how he'd been fighting with the animal for over an hour, trying to get him into a stall." Uncle Dale glanced in my direction again. "He said a two-by-four finally did the convincing, and was bragging about how he broke the donkey's ear and knocked his eye clean out of his head."

I gasped and clutched my stomach as though I'd been hit myself. Tears filled my eyes.

"Oh, dear God," Mama cried.

"Oh, Dale!" Aunt Betty said as she went to Liberty's side and gently touched his face. "I remember that. I remember how upset you were when you came home and told me about it. Do you think this is the same donkey?"

"I'll bet it is," said Uncle Dale. "How many white donkeys do you see with a broken ear and missing an eye?"

I hugged Liberty Biscuit's head to my chest and cupped my hand over his good eye, gently closing the lid. "I will never let anything happen to you, ever again," I whispered. "I promise. You are safe with me."

chapter 4

*O*ur luck was running high. When Grandpa Joe opened the door to the well-house and flipped the power switch, it whirred to life. We attached a hose to the spigot, turned the valve, and *whoosh*...out flowed crystal-clear cold water.

Liberty Biscuit brayed his approval, making us laugh. We never worried about putting him behind a fence. He rarely took his eye off me and followed every step I took, including back and forth to the Homestead while Grandpa Joe and I prepared for the arrival of the horses.

I scrubbed out two water troughs and dragged them into the half-acre enclosure where we planned to put the horses. It would provide them with enough room to move around while they regained their health and Judge Andrews considered their case. We spent two days prying good boards off the fence line of an adjacent paddock, and then we used them to replace rotten boards in what we decided to call the "Home Paddock."

There was new life and a cheerful lightness in Grandpa Joe I hadn't seen since Grandma Pearl died. He whistled and sang and told silly jokes just like he used to.

As Grandpa Joe mowed the grass in the Home Paddock, I could hear him singing over the din of the engine. I smiled my heart out as I used loppers and a handsaw to cut away the overgrown weeds and small trees growing up along the barn. Daddy was right, we couldn't even open the doors. When I finally got all the overgrowth cut away, I tried to shove the huge cross-buck doors along their tracks. One of them got stuck halfway.

I stepped back to see what might have it hung up. There wasn't anything visible from the ground. There was, however, a single door up in the loft, directly above the double cross-buck doors. I figured I'd be able to see into the track from there.

I quickly ran out to where Grandpa was mowing. He stopped and cut the engine. One of our rules while we worked around the Homestead was to always tell each other where we were working and what we were doing. Everything was so rundown and neglected, we didn't want to risk getting injured and the other person not realizing something had happened.

"I need to go up to the loft," I told him. "There's something caught in the track of the double doors. I can probably reach whatever it is from above. Think the floor up there is safe?"

"Oh, absolutely," Grandpa nodded. "I was actually up there just a few days ago. It's solid as a rock." Then he rubbed his bad knee. "Just be careful on the ladder. It's steep. I may build actual stairs up to the loft one day."

"Okay," I said and started to turn away. But something had been on my mind and I decided to ask right then. "Grandpa, why didn't you ever tell me you came over here now and then?"

"Oh, I don't know, Kipper." He frowned for a second. "I guess I just needed to be alone over here. Sometimes a body just needs to be alone with their memories." He looked away and the mower roared back to life.

I pondered his words as I slipped into the barn. The wooden ladder to the loft was built against the outside wall of the tack room. And Grandpa was right; it was nearly straight-up-and-down steep. I climbed up, then took cautious steps in the dark as I headed for the far end. When I pushed open the single loft door, sunlight flooded the space while motes of dust floated through the air like silver glitter.

I lay down on my belly and hung my head over the edge to peer into the track of the stuck door below. I could see an accumulation of acorns preventing the wheels from rolling. My arm wasn't quite long enough to reach the track. I needed something to act as an extension. I pulled out my pocket knife and flipped open the blade, but I still couldn't reach the acorns.

I stood up to look around. There were a few trunks and storage bins, several dining room chairs, an old oak dresser, and some hand tools. I could see where my boots had left prints in the decades of dust. There was also a set of larger boot prints that must've been Grandpa's. I noticed a stack of lumber in one corner, including a few dowels, which would be perfect to dislodge the acorns. As I went to retrieve one of the dowels, I was surprised by what appeared to be *two* sets of boot prints in the dust besides mine.

I stepped out of the line of light coming through the loft door and tipped my head to the side. Some of the dust was scuffed around. There was one area where those other sets of boot prints were facing each other, like two people talking. I walked over to them, and careful not to disturb the dust, I set my foot down inside one of the prints. It was drastically bigger than my size six. Definitely Grandpa's. I pivoted around and set my foot in the other print. It was bigger than mine, but smaller than the other print.

I wondered who had been up here with Grandpa Joe. Something told me not to ask him about it. He'd specifically said he'd come over here alone. There had to be be a reason he hadn't mentioned the other person.

Grabbing a dowel, I went back to the loft door and easily pushed the acorns out of the track. I rolled over onto my back and sat up. I stayed that way for a few minutes while I thought about that other set of prints. I had no way of knowing if they belonged to a woman or a man. The soles of cowboy boots don't look any different than the soles of cow*girl* boots. And all of us owned boots for working around the farm. Even Mama.

As I sat there on the floor, thinking, I rolled the dowel back and forth under my flattened hand. The thunkity-thunk tapping sound it made as it went across the uneven wooden planks was oddly soothing. It reminded me of Liberty Biscuit's awkward gait. He was a genuine blessing. His presence in our family had changed our lives and set in motion events I never could have imagined. Namely, Grandpa Joe and I over here fixing up the old barn for two starving horses who needed care.

I gave the dowel a little flick, then leaned forward to grab it as it rolled away. When I did, I could see the dust had been displaced in front of one of the old trunks. I glanced out the loft door. Liberty Biscuit was dozing in the shade of an oak tree. I watched as Grandpa Joe made a pass with the mower.

I looked back over at the trunk. When I stood in front of it, I could see the top was clean, as if someone had recently wiped the dust off. I touched the latch. It wasn't locked. My hand hovered there as the sound of Grandpa whistling drifted up to me from below. Slowly, I lifted the lid. The hinges creaked and I was hit with a musty odor—like wet towels that had sat on the bathroom floor too long.

I wasn't quite sure what to make of what I saw inside.

A faded black and white photograph of my daddy stared up at me. It sat right there on top of several boxes, worn stuffed animals, and some unidentified items wrapped in tissue paper. He looked to be about fifteen or sixteen years old, but I had no doubt it was Daddy. His mop of wavy hair, that dimple in his left cheek, and his lopsided grin gave him away.

There was another boy in the photo. A bit older. He had the same curly hair and the same wide grin. They were each on a horse. And they were both smiling so broadly you could've put them in the dictionary to define the word *ecstatic*.

So, there was a time when Daddy loved horses. The words Grandpa Joe spoke to Daddy just a few days ago came back to me: "*Get over this foolish objection you have to horses,*" and "*Let it go, son.*" I picked up the photograph and turned it over. I recognized Grandma Pearl's handwriting.

Charlie, 16 on Indigo and Henry, 18 on Padre

Henry. Who was Henry? A cousin? A neighbor? I'd never heard anyone in our family mention someone named Henry. I stared at the faces of both boys. They looked too much alike not to be related. Daddy's brother? How could that be? I frowned and shook my head. If Daddy had a brother, what happened to him? And why hadn't anyone talked about him over the years? We talk about Grandma Pearl all the time with joy in our hearts as we keep her memory alive. If this boy named Henry had died, why wouldn't everyone want to keep *his* memory alive?

The sound of the mower stopped. I placed the photo back in the trunk and quietly closed the lid. Hurrying to the loft door, I tried to ease the look of concern off my face.

"There were acorns in the track," I called down to Grandpa. "I think I got 'em all out. See how the door rolls along now."

I watched from above as Grandpa gave the big cross-buck door an easy shove. It opened fully. He offered me a thumbs-up and said, "Good job," then smiled and nodded, and added, "Kip, I think we're ready for horses."

"I'm going to wash up," Grandpa Joe said when we got back to the farm.

Mama and Daddy were in the kitchen. I could hear them talking as I took my boots off in the mudroom. I watched them for a moment from the doorway. Daddy was leaning back against the counter, his hands resting lightly on the edge. One foot was casually crossed over the other. His head was turned, his eyes on Mama as she chopped some scallions.

I studied his face as I thought about the photograph I'd found in the loft of the barn. My mind was in turmoil, wanting to ask questions, but not daring to risk disturbing the calm and contentment that had recently come back to our family.

It was strange to see Mama doing all the things that Grandma Pearl used to do. This kitchen was Grandma Pearl's domain, but she called it the "Keeping Room." It was the biggest room in our home and ran the entire length of the back of the house. On one side was our long family table that easily sat eight people. More if we scooched together when we had friends over, along with Grandma Kay and Grandpa Earl when they come down from Detroit.

There were shelves of books and knickknacks on that side of the room, and a large hutch sat behind the table. There was even space for an upholstered rocking chair where Grandma Pearl used to sit in between cooking and baking and canning. "Put my feet up for a spell," she'd say.

In the middle of the room was the actual kitchen area. The big center island had four stools in front of it. That's where I always sat after school while Grandma Pearl made me a snack, and we'd chat about what sort of day we both were having.

The other side of the Keeping Room was my favorite place. It had a large window seat with a padded bench that looked out over the garden and the woods beyond. A square oak table sat in front of the bench. Matching chairs with seat cushions were on the other three sides of the table. It's where we ate supper every evening. Well...it's where we *used to* sit. Since Grandma Pearl died, it seemed like we were all going in different directions.

"Hey, Kip," Daddy said when he saw me.

I lifted my hand in a wave and sat down at the center island.

Mama turned. "Oh, you look hot, my child."

She came over to me and put her hand on my cheek. It felt cool and soft as velvet, and I could smell the scallions she'd been chopping. The scent was fresh and enticing, and reminded me

I was hungry. Mama moved her hand to the back of my neck, lifting the sweaty-damp hair off my skin. She ran her fingers along my scalp; the pleasure of it made me close my eyes.

"You need to put your hair up when you're working outside," she said. "You got a hairband on you?"

I shook my head. She gathered my shoulder-length curls to the top of my head, then removed the mother-of-pearl clip holding her own hair and used it to secure mine into a ponytail.

"There," she murmured. "That'll feel better."

Because Mama and Daddy both have curly hair, I ended up with a double dose. Mama's hair is black as a raven's wing and grows below her shoulders. If she turns just right in the sun you can see streaks of a mysterious blue color bordering on purple. Daddy's hair is reddish blond with touches of grey. My hair color is closer to Daddy's, but more of a reddish ash-brown with streaks of sun-bleached blond.

Mama kissed my forehead. "Do you want some lemonade?"

"Oh, yes, please," I answered.

"Where's Grandpa?" she asked, opening a cupboard and reaching in for two glasses.

"Gettin' a shower."

"How's it going over there?" Daddy asked.

"Good," I said with a nod. "Grandpa says we're ready for the horses."

Daddy only nodded back.

"You should come see how everything looks." Daddy hadn't stopped by the barn once since Grandpa and I began clearing and making repairs.

Daddy lifted one shoulder in a half-shrug and mumbled, "Soon."

I was too tired to question his resistance. Mama set two glasses of lemonade down on the island, one in front of me and one in front of the empty stool beside me. Then she turned back to the counter and resumed the conversation she and Daddy were having when I walked in. But, if you asked me, I couldn't tell you what they were talking about.

Grandpa and I had worked hard that day. The sun was beginning to set, but Mama hadn't turned on any of the bright overhead work lights. The comfort of the room made me feel like I was drifting. I don't know if it was because I was overheated or overtired or both, but the individual words Mama and Daddy spoke seemed to meld together into one lilting rhythm. Their voices floated around me like I was underwater. It felt soothing and deliberate, as though nothing should disturb the moment.

I watched Mama use the wide blade of the knife to scoop the diced scallions into a skillet. She was looking down at her task while she continued to relay her story to Daddy. The tenderness in his eyes as he listened to her speak made my heart feel warm. They both chuckled over some part of Mama's story. Mama washed her hands, then dried them on a hand towel. She flipped the towel over her shoulder and reached for a bottle of olive oil, then dribbled a small amount into the black pan. Daddy said something in a teasing tone of voice. Mama laughed and whipped the towel at Daddy's stomach. He dodged the snap of the towel as he quickly grabbed her wrist, then tucked her arm back around his waist, pulling her close.

Mama was slender and petite. I got the Baker height and was already an inch taller than her. She had to tip her head back to look at Daddy's face. He leaned down and whispered something in her ear while he fingered one of her raven-black corkscrew curls and gently tugged it into a straight line. She smiled up at him, then put her cheek against his chest. Daddy kissed the top of her head.

This was normal stuff between those two and I was used to it. Grandma Pearl used to call Mama and Daddy, "The Love Birds." Seeing the affection they had for each other made me feel safe. I also loved the contrasting color of their skin. Daddy's light-colored hand on Mama's dark cheek. Mama's bare dark arm linked through Daddy's light one when they hugged.

Grandma Kay calls our two families a mixed bag of nuts, which makes me laugh. She says Grandpa Earl is the color of a brazil nut. She herself says she's the color of an almond.

Mama's skin is the color of a pecan, which Daddy says is perfect, "'cause she's a southern girl now." Daddy, Grandma Pearl, and Grandpa Joe are the white color of the flesh of a cashew. And me, I'm a mixture of them all. Grandma Kay says my skin is the color of a walnut. If I was going to be referred to as a nut, I would've preferred a more attractive shell than a wrinkly old walnut, but there it is. Our mixed bag of nuts.

"Kip." Daddy's voice pulled me from my dream state. "C'mere," he said, motioning me to come between him and Mama. Mama smiled and held out her arm.

I made a "p'shaw" sound and waved my hands at them. "I don't need to get between all that sugar," I said.

Daddy broke away from Mama and rushed at me. He grabbed me in a hug while he tickled my ribs, saying, "Gettin' too big for sugar, are ya?"

"Stop!" I hollered, laughing and twisting to get away from him. "I just didn't want to get in the middle of all that...sticky-icky mess."

"Sticky-icky mess?" Daddy said in a dramatically shocked tone of voice. I laughed at the expression on his face. "You hear that, Elise? She called us a sticky-icky mess!"

"I heard her," Mama said with a "isn't that child shameful?" cluck of her tongue. But she was smiling and had gone back to preparing the meal.

Daddy went back to leaning against the counter but pointed his finger at me. "Just don't ever forget you'll always be my baby girl, and your old daddy needs a hug now and then."

I rolled my eyes and sat back down to drink my lemonade.

"And speaking of sticky-icky messes," Daddy said, "if the fencing is done over there at the homestead and you got the water running, it's time for you to start leaving your donkey in the paddock."

"Oh, Daddy. I can't leave Liberty Biscuit over there alone."

"And why not?"

"Because *love*, that's why. We love each other. He needs me and I need him."

Daddy scowled in a comical way, then crossed his arms over his chest. "Well, I'm tired of him hanging out on the porch, waiting for you to come out. And this braying when you *don't* come out is getting mighty tiresome."

Just then we heard, *clomp, clomp, clomp,* up the steps of the porch. My sweet donkey had an uncanny knack for doing exactly what Daddy didn't want him to do at the exact moment Daddy spoke the words. The clomping continued along the porch till we saw his precious face in the lower windows over by the nook where we eat. He brayed when he saw me. Naturally.

Mama laughed. Daddy rolled his eyes.

"Liberty Biscuit!" I called. "Go graze!"

We all heard him sigh through the screen. Exasperated by human foolishness, I'm certain.

"And why does he wait till he's on the porch to relieve himself?"

"I clean it up," I said. "Besides, he doesn't do it very often."

"The stains are easy to hose off," Mama added.

"That's not the po—," Daddy began, but he was cut off by the sound of Liberty Biscuit groaning, followed by the sound of plopping. And then a distinctive odor wafted through the window. I did not find this odor offensive.

Daddy's chin dropped to his chest while Mama's head fell backward and she practically howled with laughter. I searched the floor for a distraction.

"What's so funny?" Grandpa Joe asked, stepping into the kitchen. His thick grey hair was neatly combed and still wet from the shower. He was wearing a pair of blue jean shorts and a short-sleeve blue and white plaid shirt. I thought he looked handsome.

Mama wiped the tears of laughter from her eyes as she pointed at the window where Liberty was still standing.

"We were just about to invite Liberty Biscuit in to join us for supper," Daddy said.

"Why, thank you, Daddy," I said in a fake-sweet tone of voice as I pushed away from the island and got up, pretending to head for the door so Liberty could come inside. I knew Daddy was being sarcastic, but Mama was so tickled by the conversation I couldn't help teasing him.

Daddy pointed at me and said, "You're funny. You're a funny girl."

I took a bow. "Thank you. Thank you very much. I'll be here all week."

That made everybody laugh, including Daddy, even though he was not happy about Liberty's presence on the porch.

Mama was still chuckling and dabbing at her eyes when she said, "I poured you a lemonade, Joe."

Grandpa Joe sat down beside me. "Thank you, Elise," he said. "That looks good." Then, "Do I smell manure?"

Mama and I burst into another fit of laughter. Once we had settled back down, Mama asked me to set the table. I took four plates from the cupboard and noticed Mama slicing an apple. She joined me in the nook. I was shocked to see her sit down and pluck the screen out of the window. Then she sat there just as pleased as can be, passing slices of apple to Liberty.

"Mama!" I exclaimed as my eyes darted to Daddy. Believe it or not, he and Grandpa Joe didn't even notice. They were lost in conversation about the goings-on of the farm while Liberty chomped apples and drooled juice all over the sill.

When the slices were gone, he poked his head all the way into the kitchen, searching for more. Then he must have smelled the juice on the sill. He leaned down and licked the wood. Mama held one finger up to her lips to quiet me as we both did everything we could to keep from laughing out loud. Suddenly, Liberty chomped the sill. His teeth left a half-moon indentation in the wood.

I gasped.

Mama said, "Ooops!"

Daddy said, "What in the world!"

Grandpa Joe laughed.

And Liberty Biscuit brayed.

Mama stood up and waved her hands at Daddy like she was trying to disperse smoke. "Nothing to see here," she said. "Go back to what you were talking about." Then she pushed Liberty's head out of the kitchen and set the screen back into its track.

She rubbed her hand over the teeth marks and whispered, "They'll never notice. Besides, it adds character." I felt so proud seeing that Mama clearly loved this raggedy little donkey as much as I did.

She and I finished setting the table, then Mama gave my hand a little squeeze and very quietly said, "I want you to sit in Grandma Pearl's spot this evening."

I crinkled my brow and mouthed the word, "Why," as I stole a quick glance at Grandpa Joe. He and Daddy had gone back to their conversation.

"Because," Mama said, still speaking quietly, "it's time to create a new normal for Grandpa. We need to break the routine of everybody sitting where they always sit. Right now, the only thing sitting in Grandma Pearl's chair is grief. It's time to fill her chair with your smiling face."

I just stared at Mama for a minute, trying to absorb what she was saying. She put her hand on my cheek. "Okay?" she said. I nodded.

I went back to sit beside Grandpa while Mama finished making supper.

This was the first evening in a very long time we had all been in the Keeping Room at the same time. It was the first time all of us had laughed, really laughed, in a very long time. I tried not to let my eyes drift over to Grandma Pearl's empty rocker.

chapter 5

I feared my heart was going to beat right out of my chest as Sheriff Ronnie backed the stock trailer up to our barn. I could see the two horses through the side rails; they appeared nervous. I could actually see the whites of their eyes. Their heads were high and their nostrils flared. One of them hollered out a plaintive call. Liberty Biscuit must have recognized the voice of his friend. He ran circles around the truck and trailer, bucking and braying.

"They look scared," I said to Grandpa Joe as we watched from the fence line.

Grandpa put his arm around my shoulders. "Unfamiliar surroundings can be stressful for horses," he said.

"We'll get them unloaded and give them all the time they need to settle in."

Sheriff Ronnie positioned the back doors of the trailer at the opening to the aisleway, then cut the engine of his dually pickup. He came over and extended a hand to Grandpa.

"I sure appreciate this, Joe," he said as the two men shook. He turned to me. "You, too, Kip."

But I barely heard him. I couldn't take my eyes off the horses inside the trailer. Neither could Liberty Biscuit. He had tipped his nose up to one of the horses and tried to sniff him through the opening between the rails.

"Glad to help," Grandpa said. "More than glad, truth be told. I've missed horses."

Sheriff Ronnie put his hand on my shoulder to get my attention. I looked up at him. "Before we unload them," he said, "I need you to know they haven't been handled much. Neither one has a mean bone in his body, they just have no use for humans. They're difficult to work with, even getting a halter on or off them isn't easy. So, Kip? Promise me you'll listen to your grandpa and stay safe."

"Yes, sir," I said, bobbing my head up and down. "I promise."

"I haven't seen a bit of aggressive behavior, Joe," Sheriff Ronnie said to Grandpa. "They aren't dangerous in that way. But they don't want to be caught. And they're fearful of being touched once they are caught. Especially the black." He shifted his eyes back to where I stood. "So, they aren't horses that you should handle."

I turned back to the trailer. My eyes sought which one Sheriff Ronnie referred to as the black. But the two geldings looked identical in the dark confines of the trailer. I could hear their hooves shuffling impatiently on the wooden floor.

"Why don't we get them into stalls so we can remove their halters?" Grandpa said. "Then we can turn them out to the paddock. I don't want to turn them out with halters on."

Sheriff Ronnie nodded. "Sounds good," he said.

"Kip, go open two stall doors from the aisleway, but leave the exit doors to the paddock closed. Then you get behind the center gate. Make sure it's latched tight, and let us know when you're ready."

I ran to do as I was asked.

"All set," I called once I was behind the gate that split the long aisleway in two.

"We're gonna open the trailer doors now," Grandpa said.

I watched Sheriff Ronnie and Grandpa Joe each grab onto the latches of the two back doors. They swung them both open at the same time. The horses, loose inside, pivoted in unison but stopped at the edge, snorted, dipped their heads, then cautiously stepped down together. Immediately, their heads shot back up as they surveyed the barn and their new surroundings.

I could see now that one of the geldings was dark bay—a rich brown color with a black mane and tail and lower legs. The other was a true black—no brown or red hints anywhere on his coat. Their ribs were showing and their hip bones stuck out. The bay kept his shoulder in contact with the black. They high-stepped up to the gate where I was standing, watching them. I felt their breath on my face as my own breath caught in my lungs. I was in such awe, tears stung my eyes. The two horses reeled away from me, and faced with the trailer blocking their exit, they filed into one of the open stalls.

"Easy, boys," Grandpa whispered as he gently closed the stall door. "Easy."

The horses circled the twelve-by-twelve box, bedded deep with the shavings I'd scattered the day before. Grandpa backed away to the far side of the aisle, giving them space. I watched as he angled his shoulders away from them and lowered his eyes. It didn't take long for the horses to quiet, but their eyes stayed wide, etched with worry.

"Let's bring Liberty Biscuit into the aisle," Grandpa said.

Sheriff Ronnie got in his truck and pulled the trailer away from the barn. Liberty Biscuit ran right in as soon as the opening was clear. He trotted up to the half-wall of the stall where his friends were standing, extending their necks into the aisle. All three of them seemed so happy to see one another, touching noses and snuffling each other as the two horses nickered. My heart swelled over the reunion. Grandpa Joe waited, then slowly stepped forward. The black quickly backed away. Grandpa put his arm around Liberty and scratched his neck. Liberty leaned against Grandpa. The black watched. Then the bay leaned forward and sniffed Grandpa's hand. Grandpa rolled his hand sideways, and his fingers gently curled around the bay's halter. In one motion, Grandpa released the throat latch and slipped the halter off his head.

Grandpa hung the halter on a hook in the aisleway, then quietly opened the stall door and stepped inside. Both horses backed into a far corner. Once again, Grandpa softly said, "Easy, boys. Easy, now." He relaxed his shoulders and lowered his eyes, then moved toward them.

"Move up," he said. "Nice and easy. Move up." The horses moved out of the corner. Grandpa stayed behind them and continued to ask for a few steps forward. Then he changed direction and stood directly in front of them. The horses didn't move. Their eyes were riveted on Grandpa. He stepped between them. The black backed away. Grandpa lowered his eyes and turned sideways, angled away from the black, and reached for his shoulder. The tall horse's skin quivered when Grandpa touched him, but he stayed still.

I could tell the black would be truly gorgeous once he regained his health. Both horses would be, but especially the black.

"Easy," Grandpa repeated in a low voice. He moved his hand up the black's neck. Then, just as he'd done with the bay, he curled his fingers through the halter. The black jerked his head when he felt pressure, but not hard enough for Grandpa to lose hold. Grandpa released the throat latch and slipped it over the black's head.

I was mesmerized watching Grandpa Joe. I knew he was good with horses, but I didn't realize it would be pure magic to see.

"Nice work," Sheriff Ronnie said from where he stood in the doorway.

"Let's let these two boys stretch their legs," Grandpa said.

He opened the exit door to the paddock. Both horses bolted out of the stall and broke into a pounding run, belying their state of starvation. Liberty Biscuit brayed and ran a zigzag along the aisleway, searching for a way to join his friends. But before we could let him into the stall to follow the horses, he ran out of the barn and along the fence line of the paddock. I quickly went to the paddock gate and called to him. He trotted to my side, waited for me to open it, then dashed through.

We couldn't help but laugh at the sight of the little white Liberty Biscuit with his awkward trot alongside the graceful motion of the two dark horses.

"I can't believe this," I said. My hands rested along the top rail of the fence. I couldn't seem to stop the happy tears in my eyes. "I simply can't believe it, Grandpa." He came to stand beside me. He put his arm around me, but never took his eyes off the horses.

"There's something indescribable about them, isn't there?"

We didn't want to leave, but it was time to head back to the house. I opened the gate to the paddock, inviting Liberty to come along with us, just as he did every day since his arrival.

The following morning, Grandpa Joe and I quickly ate our breakfast. We wanted to get over to the horses. Mama was already outside, hanging her weekly load of clean sheets and bedding on the clothesline. We had a dryer, but Mama preferred drying our laundry in the sun.

Once Grandpa Joe and I did our dishes, we were ready to head to the Homestead. When we walked outside, though, we were shocked to discover Liberty dancing and twirling in the clean white linens Mama had just hung out to dry. I ran to collect him, but before I could he'd twisted himself into one of the sheets and pulled it right off the line. Then he began strutting around like royalty on coronation day. Unfortunately, in his merry enthusiasm, he stomped the sheet into the dirt.

Mama was extremely tolerant of Liberty's shenanigans, even aiding and abetting from time to time, but this was too much.

She did, however, gather up the evidence before Daddy caught sight.

chapter 6

Kip," Grandpa Joe said. "One of the best ways to work with a horse who doesn't want to be handled is to not work with him at all."

"What does that mean?" I asked.

We were in the tack room of the barn where Grandpa used to store saddles and bridles and halters and everything else you needed to tend horses. I loved the honey-colored walls. They were made of tongue-and-groove pine boards. I envisioned all the empty shelves full of grooming supplies and all the racks full of gear, just like back when the Homestead was active with horses. Although Grandpa and I were spending just about every minute of daylight over here, we hadn't devoted much attention to the inside of the barn. Our focus had been the fencing and clearing the paddock.

"When a horse is scared because he's been mistreated or he simply hasn't been handled much, like these two," Grandpa said with a glance toward the paddock, "give him time to get used to the sound of your voice and the way you smell. Give him time to become familiar with your body language."

Grandpa was sweeping the tack-room floor while we talked. The *swish, swish* of the broom matched the tempo of his words. "Every horse should be allowed the dignity of participating in his own life. He should be allowed to make decisions. He has a right to his own life beyond serving mankind." Grandpa stopped sweeping for a moment. "Give horses a reason to be curious about you, Kip. So they want to be with you."

I'll never forget these words, I thought. *And I'll never forget how blessed and lucky I am to have Grandpa Joe in my life.*

The first thing we did every morning after eating breakfast was pack a cooler with snacks and a few sandwiches for lunch.

Then we'd load up the farm's ATV—the all-terrain vehicle, which was sort of like a golf cart on steroids—and take off down the path between home and the barn. I'd been driving the ATV since I could reach the pedals.

I had decided Liberty Biscuit was better off staying with the horses at night, especially after the unfortunate incident with Mama's laundry. He was quite content to remain with his friends, but as soon as he heard the motor of the ATV, before we even came into view, his trumpeting bray would reverberate across the property. And the moment he saw me, he would run to the fence line like his heels were on fire. I would always scramble through the boards and hug his head to my chest while I cupped my hand over his good eye, gently shutting his lid.

I loved that scraggly little donkey. He filled that excruciating yearning in my heart for a pet of my own.

When he and the horses had been with us for just over a month, they began to look much better, thanks to Grandpa's knowledge and our daily care. All three were beginning to put on weight. Their ribs and hip bones didn't stick out nearly as bad as when they'd arrived. They grazed the large paddock and we invited them each into their own stall several times a day to eat small, nutritional meals. Grandpa said you couldn't feed a starved horse big meals. It was too hard on their internal organs.

One afternoon, Sheriff Ronnie sent Doc Sam out to document their progress for the court case. The vet draped her stethoscope around her neck as she hopped out of her truck. We already had the horses in their own stalls, ready for her. Doc Sam was small, but she was also very fit and strong. I guess you had to be if you wanted to be a vet for farm animals. She was wearing cowboy boots and jeans. Her shirt was the same kind that nurses wear in hospitals—"scrubs"—with her name and clinic logo embroidered above the pocket. Her long brown hair was pulled into a pony tail high on top of her head.

Doc Sam and Grandpa shook hands. She looked over at me and said, "Hi, Kip. Are you enjoying all the work that goes along with having horses?"

"Yes, ma'am," I answered. "I sure am."

"Well, it looks like you and your grandpa are doing a great job," she said as she stepped over to the stall where we'd put the bay gelding. "Joe, is it okay if I get some vitals on these two?"

"Absolutely," Grandpa Joe replied. He opened the stall door and gently clipped a lead line on the bay's halter. The horse seemed a bit concerned as Grandpa held him, but he stood still for Doc Sam. She used her stethoscope to listen to his heart and his lungs. Then she listened to his stomach.

She straightened, then looked at Grandpa Joe. "Is it okay if Kip comes into the stall?"

"Sure," Grandpa said.

"Here, Kip," Doc Sam said handing me her stethoscope. "Put this on." Curious, I did as she asked, tucking my hair behind my ears as I inserted the ear pieces. Then Doc Sam held up the other end of the stethoscope and said, "This is called the 'bell.'" She pressed it against the bay's stomach. My mouth dropped open over the noises I heard as my wide eyes shifted from the bell to Doc Sam. "Cool, huh?" she said with a smile.

"Is he okay?" I asked.

"He sure is. That's called *borborygmus*. Or as we professionals like to say, 'gut sounds.'" She laughed. I did, too. "That pinging and groaning you hear means good bacteria is breaking down food in the cecum—a part of his digestive system—so he can absorb the nutrition, utilize the fiber, then eliminate the rest."

"Wow," I said as I handed back her stethoscope. Grandpa Joe was smiling big.

Doc Sam continued the exam. She looked in the bay's mouth and his ears. She ran her hands down all four legs. She walked all the way around him, touching him everywhere. She then did the same with the black, who fidgeted worriedly the entire time, but she moved slowly and Grandpa talked softly to him in a calming way.

When she was done with the exams, Doc Sam and Grandpa talked for a few moments. She told us again that we were doing a commendable job. She held up her clipboard as she explained that she'd write up a report for Judge Andrews and give a copy to Sheriff Ronnie. Then the vet lifted her hand in a friendly wave as she climbed into her truck and drove away.

The bay gelding had come to accept our touch, but the black still kept his distance. If we raised our hand, slow and gentle, or extended our arm in his direction, he bolted in fear. Grandpa was alarmed by all the scars on his head. That, coupled with his fear of his head being touched, convinced Grandpa the black had been repeatedly hit on the head.

When we got the black into a stall as we had today, lured by his daily meals, we would slip the halter gently on and off so he'd become accustomed to the motion. Eventually he'd come to allow us to run our hands all over his body, just like Doc Sam had, as we made every effort to reassure him we weren't going to hurt him. But when he was loose in the paddock, he wouldn't let us within six feet. We didn't push him, though, so every day seemed a bit better.

Grandpa brought his guitar over to the Homestead. He'd never had any formal lessons, but had taught himself to play on an old Gibson he found at a junk shop before I was born. He didn't know any actual songs. He made up his own tunes by stringing simple chords together. They sounded pretty terrific to me. Sometimes he added lyrics that were just as made up as the tunes themselves. When he stumbled over what words to use or couldn't think of any, he filled in the blanks by singing, "Ba-dum, ba-dum, ba-dum-dum-dum."

This made me laugh and laugh because he acted like these were perfectly acceptable, actual words.

"In the gl-o-o-o-w of the setting s-u-u-u-n, ba-dum, ba-dum, the ba-dum gather..."

That was most likely what you'd find us doing in the afternoon; sitting in a couple of lawn chairs in the shade of the barn, watching Liberty Biscuit and the horses graze while Grandpa played the guitar.

One day Grandpa and I were sitting just like that, and he was strumming the guitar as we sang silly nonsense and laughed at the songs we made up. Suddenly, Grandpa looked over my shoulder and abruptly stopped playing.

"What's wrong?" I asked.

"Shhh," he said putting one finger to his lips. Then he nodded, motioning for me to look behind me. I slowly turned my head sideways to discover the black taking cautious steps in our direction. The big horse came within a few inches of where I sat. He stretched his neck down and snuffled my hair. My eyes got big as saucers. I resisted the urge to jump up and hug his neck.

Grandpa smiled. He softly strummed the guitar and sang, "Oh, it's a ba-dump-idy dum day when a horse says hey. Ba-dum, ba-dum, a great, great day."

And boy, was it ever a great day. I tipped my head back so I could see the black's eyes and whispered, "That's all we want, fella. We just wanna be friends."

I felt his breath on the back of my neck and a shiver of happiness ran along my arms, even though we were into August and it was as hot and steamy as ever. The black touched my shoulder with his velvet-soft nose, then casually strolled away.

Grandpa stopped playing. "That's exactly the way you want to help a horse learn to trust, Kipper. Let him come to you. His curiosity about us got the best of him, and now he knows he can come close and he won't be harmed."

"I can't believe it," I said and shook my head in awe. Then I felt my expression change to a frown. "Why do people hurt horses, Grandpa?"

"Aww, Kip." He paused. "Ego, ignorance, a glitch in their psyche. I dunno. There's been evil in the world since the beginning of time, I suspect there always will be." Grandpa reached over and patted my knee. "But ya know what? There's an awful lot of good in the world, too. Always search for the good, Kipper."

I blinked a few times, thinking about his words. *Always search for the good.* Then I asked, "When are we going to give the horses names?"

"Maybe we better wait on that," Grandpa replied quietly. "It might be harder to let them go if we give them special names and then the judge decides to let their old owner have them back."

I shuddered when I thought about that possibility.

"What about Liberty Biscuit, Grandpa?" I asked, concern flooding my body. "I...I don't know what I'll do if..." My voice trailed off and I felt my throat tighten with emotion.

"Let's not worry about things before they happen, Kipper," Grandpa said as he pulled me into a hug.

I buried my face in his chest. "I couldn't stand it, Grandpa." I was trying not to cry, but a sob squeaked out. "I love that little boy."

"I know you do," Grandpa said. "And he loves you." Grandpa gave me a squeeze, then gently pulled back from our embrace. "How about we drive along the back fence line of the property? Check for any repairs that might need to be made? It won't be long before these guys will be healthy enough to have the run of the whole place."

I nodded. I knew he was trying to get my mind off the possibility of losing the horses...and losing Liberty Biscuit.

"You drive," Grandpa instructed.

We hopped in the ATV and headed off across the pasture. Grandpa and I had already repaired the fence that came off the barn and ran along the north side of the fifty-acre Homestead. It was a short run of wire and there hadn't been much to do. I slowed the ATV to a crawl as we approached the western fence line. It divided the old Homestead from our home and the orchards, along with the heavy woods between the two places and right up to the perimeter of the south and east sides of the acreage. To the north were more woods, then Busby Creek, and then the Savannah River beyond.

Past our property line was a two-thousand-acre tree farm owned by a timber company, technically referred to as a "planted pine plantation." *Ooof.* Say that fast three times.

The woods growing heavily into the fence line actually worked to our advantage. The brush and overgrowth were so thick they held the original metal posts and wire together. It didn't look pretty, but it would be nearly impossible for a horse to breach. And really, as Grandpa pointed out, there would be no reason for the horses to try to break through—as long as they had food and water, and the companionship of each other, and they didn't feel threatened.

"This will save us a lot of work, won't it, Grandpa?" I said, thinking about his bad knee.

"It sure will," he replied. "A good thing, with my poor old knee acting up. Not sure I could do much serious fencing right now."

We came to the far boundary of the property. I turned the ATV left to cruise along the south side. This was the longest line of fence, but our luck held. The woods were just as dense here, and the wire fencing was just as wound up and tangled with overgrowth, creating a sturdy barrier.

Grandpa and I looked at each other and nodded, both of us pleased. When we got to the southeast corner, I turned left, once again. Just as we got about halfway along the eastern fence line, I saw something that didn't seem right. I slowed the ATV to a stop.

"What's wrong?" Grandpa asked.

I set the brake. "Is that a path?" I pointed into the woods.

Grandpa leaned left, then right peering through the trees. "Might be a deer trail," he replied with a shrug. "They tend to walk the same route to water and food plots."

"It's awful wide for a deer trail," I said. "The ATV would nearly fit."

Once again, Grandpa just shrugged, so I let it go and continued on till we made our way back to the barn.

"The entire pasture looks secure," Grandpa said with relief. "We lucked out, Kipper."

"Yes, sir, we sure did." I smiled at him.

"How about we bring the big tractor and the brush hog over here tomorrow and get this area mowed?" Grandpa suggested.

"Sounds good," I agreed.

chapter 7

The hot days of July had crept into the steamy days of August. Grandpa Joe and I drove the ATV home after feeding the horses. As we got closer to the house, we could see Sheriff Ronnie's dually pickup in our driveway. He and Daddy were standing near the porch. Mama was on the steps, one hip leaned against the railing. I didn't think too much of it. Sheriff Ronnie had stopped by several times over the last few weeks to check on the horses.

But then I got a better look at Mama's face. She was frowning and her mouth was twisted to the side. One arm was across her stomach and her other hand was clutching at her throat in a nervous way. When her eyes met mine, she blinked rapidly a few times, then looked away.

I cut the engine of the ATV and went to where they stood. For some reason, Grandpa stayed seated.

"What's wrong?" I asked, because I knew something was.

Daddy ran his hand roughly across his mouth, then along the back of his neck.

"Listen, Kip..." he started, but his voice trailed off.

My eyes darted over to Mama. Now I could see the tears that rimmed her lashes and threatened to spill. My heart began to pound in my chest. I felt like I couldn't breathe. I looked over at the sheriff.

"What's wrong?" I repeated, louder than I meant.

Sheriff Ronnie put his hands on his hips and looked down at the ground. "Kip," he said, inhaling deeply. "The judge returned custody of the horses to Len Parker."

"No," I said. My hands began to shake. "What about Liberty?"

"Liberty, too," Sheriff Ronnie said quietly. "Kip, I'm so sor—"

"No!" I yelled, cutting him off. I looked at Grandpa. He was clutching the roll bar of the ATV. His head was down.

"Kip," Daddy said. "You knew this was a possibility. And it's one of the main reasons I didn't want to take these animals in."

I looked at Sheriff Ronnie. "What was the excuse Len Parker gave the judge? Why were those horses starving?" I said jutting an angry finger in the direction of the Homestead.

"Parker claimed he'd fallen on bad times and was too proud to ask for help. And he claimed he...cared too much for them ...to give them up." I could tell by the way Sheriff Ronnie spoke the words, he didn't believe them any more than I did.

"What about those scars all over the black's head? Why is he so terrified of humans?"

"That horse has clearly been beaten, Ronnie," Grandpa agreed.

"And the rope burns on the legs of the bay?" I added, feeling sicker as I said the words.

Sheriff Ronnie shook his head. "None of that was admissible. Physical abuse has to be witnessed. And Parker claimed the horses just suffered normal injuries and mishaps that horses get from being turned out. There was no way to prove otherwise."

"Ronnie," Mama said. "Isn't there anything we can do?"

"I'm afraid not, Elise. Parker was ordered to pay a nominal fine and reimburse the county for the vet bills and feed and hay while the horses were stabled at the fairgrounds. Since he has come up with the funds, the horses are to be returned to his custody." Sheriff Ronnie shrugged his shoulders.

Mama shook her head and turned away.

Tears burned my eyes. I gritted my teeth so hard my jaw hurt. I felt like I'd been punched in the stomach. I was horrified. Horrified for the two geldings. But especially horrified for my little Liberty Biscuit. What would he do without me? What would we do without each other? How could this be happening?

"Kip," Sheriff Ronnie tried. His voice was kind. But I couldn't look at him, even though I knew this wasn't his fault. "One of my deputies is on his way over here with the trailer." I heard him take another deep breath. "Right now."

A gasping wretched sound escaped my throat. "It...it would be different—" I stopped. I felt like I couldn't breathe. I panted in and out. "It would be different if they hadn't been abused." My voice was choked with sobs. "You...can forgive a man for...for falling on hard times." I reached up and grabbed my head with both hands, trying to keep it from exploding. My chest was heaving as I tried to talk through the sobs. "But... but not abuse. Not...hitting a defenseless animal till he's lost an eye!"

"Kip," Daddy said. I felt his hand on my back.

"No!" I screamed and twisted out of his reach. Suddenly we heard the clatter and metal clang of a stock trailer in tow coming down our drive.

"No," I sobbed. I broke into a run in the direction of the Homestead.

I heard Daddy utter, "Dammit!"

Mama called, "Katherine!" But I didn't stop.

I was holding Liberty's head to my chest when Mama and Daddy arrived in the ATV. Grandpa wasn't with them. Sheriff Ronnie was in his truck, and his deputy pulling the trailer was behind him. My sobs had turned into hiccupping gasps.

Sheriff Ronnie came through the gate. He was holding a halter. He put his hand on my shoulder. "I'm sorry, Kip."

"Please, Ronnie," I sobbed, dispensing with the formality of calling him "Sheriff." Hoping he'd remember he was a family friend. *We were friends.* "Please don't do this. Please. That man hit Liberty till he lost his eye. He broke his ear and nearly broke his leg." I grabbed Ronnie's arm and pawed at him in desperation. "Please, don't take him back there," I sobbed. "I'm begging you. Don't take him from me."

The sheriff pried my hands off his arm. He looked back at Daddy. Daddy came to my side. I turned away and wrapped my arms around Liberty's neck. Daddy tried to pull them off.

"No, Daddy, please," I sobbed. "Don't let this happen."

I cast around for Mama. "Mama!" I called. She put her hands over her mouth and shook her head as tears streamed down her face.

Daddy gripped my arms. "There's nothing we can do, Katherine," he said.

Sheriff Ronnie slipped the halter over Liberty's head.

"No," I cried again. I shook my head from side to side. "No! Please. I'm begging you."

Sheriff Ronnie led Liberty Biscuit to the trailer. He tossed his head and bucked a few times. The deputy opened the trailer doors. Sheriff Ronnie stepped inside. He gave the lead rope a tug. Liberty tossed his head again and leaned back. The deputy got behind Liberty and pushed while Sheriff Ronnie pulled.

Liberty strained against the halter and twisted his head to the side. His good eye was rimmed in white as he searched for me out of fear and confusion.

"You're hurting him," I yelled. "Stop!"

Liberty lunged sideways, his body slammed against the trailer. I winced as though I'd been struck. The deputy pushed him back to the center of the open doors while the sheriff continued pulling the lead rope. I saw him quickly loop it through the slats of the trailer so he had more leverage.

Liberty's breathing had become ragged as he strained against the rope. The halter had twisted sideways, pinching his mouth.

"Stop!" I screamed. "Daddy! Make them stop!"

"Jesus, Ronnie!" Daddy yelled.

"Please, stop!" I pushed myself between the deputy and Liberty.

"Ronnie!" Daddy yelled again, reaching for the rope. "You're hurting him."

The sheriff released the pressure. He was breathing hard. His uniform shirt was stained with sweat. "Listen," he said. "I have *got* to do this. I'm not any happier than you. But I do *not* have a choice."

"Just let him calm down," Daddy said, putting his hand on Liberty's shoulder and readjusting the halter. "Let's all calm down." He looked at me.

But I couldn't calm down. I couldn't stop crying. "Please," I whimpered to Sheriff Ronnie. "Please, don't take him from me." I looked over at Daddy. "Fix this, Daddy."

"Kip, I can't fix it. We knew this might happen. There's nothing I can do."

"But I promised him. I promised him he'd never be hurt again." I wrapped my arms around Liberty's head. "I'm begging you...Daddy, fix this."

"Kip," Daddy said, shaking his head.

Suddenly, Sheriff Ronnie stepped out of the trailer. He held the lead rope out to me. I looked down at the rope, then back up into his eyes, hopeful.

"I need you to load him," he said.

"What?" I stammered.

"Charlie," he said. "I need her to load this animal. Now. Kip, please. Take this rope, get up in that trailer, and load him."

The shock of what he was asking me to do knocked the crying out of me.

"No," I said. "I won't have him believing I wanted this." I swiped my hand across my eyes in an angry gesture, wiping away the tears. Liberty leaned against me, his breathing slowly returning to normal.

"Animals don't reason that way, Kip," Sheriff Ronnie said.

"This animal does," I said. I barely recognized my own voice. If someone had held a mirror up, I bet I wouldn't have recognized the look on my face. Both were filled with panic and desperation, two things I'd never felt in my life.

Sheriff Ronnie put the lead rope in my hand. "Load him, Kip."

"No." I clenched my teeth.

I felt Daddy's hand on my back.

"Do as you're told."

"No," I growled without looking into his eyes. "I won't do it."

"This is gonna happen, Kip," Sheriff Ronnie said. "Calmly, with you. Or not so calm with me and Deputy Alan."

"Kip," Daddy said again. "Do as you're told."

My legs began to shake. I felt dizzy. I stared straight ahead, not making eye contact with anyone. Everything around me was washed in a fog. I saw no way out.

Biting the inside of my mouth, I stepped in front of Liberty. I bent down so our faces were even. "You listen to me..." I whispered. "I love you. And I am so sorry I broke my promise." I cupped my hand over his good eye, closing it for just a second. "But I'm gonna make you another promise. And this one won't be broken. I'm gonna do everything in my power to get you back. I don't know if I'll be successful, but I'm never going to stop trying."

I kissed his cheek and hugged his head a final time. "Oh, god," I sobbed, then took a few deep breaths and stepped up into the trailer. Liberty never shifted his one eye away from mine.

"I'm so sorry," I whispered. My chin quivered as I watched him bob his head, his signature nod. I nodded back. It had become a thing between us. "C'mon," I said, blinking the tears out of my eyes. "It's okay," I whispered. Nausea burned my stomach over the betrayal in my words. "C'mon," I repeated. Liberty nodded again, then he leaped inside next to me. I squeezed my eyes shut as my chest seized with silent sobs.

Sheriff Ronnie jumped up to secure the lead rope and I backed away. In a blur, the geldings were loaded, the back doors to the trailer were closed, and the latch was set in place.

The deputy climbed into the truck, the engine rumbled to life, and I watched the back of the trailer pull away and out of sight as Liberty Biscuit's agonized bray reverberated back to me through the woods.

"Charlie. Elise," Sheriff Ronnie said. "I'm truly sorry." Out of the corner of my eye, I saw him turn toward me. "Kip." I didn't move my eyes from the last spot I'd seen the trailer as it carried Liberty Biscuit away. "Kip," he repeated. "I give you my word that I will make unannounced wellness checks at Len Parker's place. If I ever have an iota of concern over the care his animals are receiving, they will be removed."

I huffed out a humorless laugh. "We all see how *that* worked out."

"They will be removed permanently," Sheriff Ronnie added ignoring my smart-alecky tone. Then he turned away and got into his truck.

Mama started walking toward me. I shook my head, stopping her. My eyes darted to Daddy. We stared at each other. I saw him swallow hard.

"Kip," he said. "You have to understand—"

"No," I hissed, taking a step backward. "I don't have to understand anything. Except that you made me betray Liberty Biscuit. That little boy *trusted* me. And I will *never* forgive you for making me load him in that trailer." I spat the words out as the sobs once again rose in my chest. "I hate you!" I screamed.

I turned and ran into the woods.

chapter 8

When I reached Busby Creek, I sat down and yanked off my boots. I wanted to throw them in the water, but I slammed them on the ground beside me instead—over and over like an angry judge pounding his gavel on the bench. When I was spent and out of breath, I fell backward and looked up at the sky.

The sun was still above the tips of the pine trees on the other side of the creek. It didn't get dark till after eight o'clock this time of year. I wondered if Liberty and the geldings were still on the road to Len Parker's or if they had already been unloaded at his ranch. Did they have clean water to drink? Fresh hay? Did they miss me and Grandpa Joe?

I knew Liberty missed me. I ached for him.

I rolled up my jeans, then strode along the shoreline till I came to my secret spot next to the water. I paced among the moss-covered rocks and boulders as the heartbreaking sound of Liberty's anguished bray, calling to me from the trailer, played over and over in my head. The horror of the day took me from grief to outrage and back again.

I sat down and leaned back against one of the larger boulders and closed my eyes. They were swollen from crying. My head throbbed. I tried to clear my thoughts, but couldn't. I was too agitated. My lungs hurt and my breaths came short and ragged. I felt disoriented. I got up and stepped back into the creek and bent over to cup a handful of water to splash my face. But when I saw my reflection, I froze.

Thirteen-year-old Kip Baker was gone.

I wondered who would take her place.

I had been sitting in my secret spot for about a half-hour, when suddenly I could hear the faint hum of the ATV cruising along the dirt lane. The sound was getting closer. I burrowed deeper in between two boulders, unwilling to reveal myself. I wasn't ready to face my family.

The ATV came to a stop a few feet from where I sat. So much for secret hiding places. The driver cut the engine. One part of me hoped it was Daddy. Another part of me hoped it wasn't. A pair of boots came into view. I lifted my chin off my drawn-up knees and looked up at Grandpa. He eased down beside me.

Neither one of us said anything. What was there to say? *Well, this certainly stinks to high heaven like a million trucks full of rotting garbage.* Or maybe, *Aren't we having an awful day.*

After a few moments, Grandpa sighed. A weary sound.

"Your daddy used to come here when he was a boy," he said. Then he made a small noise that tried to resemble a laugh. "Mostly when he was mad."

Figures, I thought, but didn't say it. Daddy and I...two peas in a pod.

"Your folks are worried about you," Grandpa said. "Can I give you a lift?"

I got up and retrieved my boots, then joined Grandpa in the ATV. He drove. My throat tightened as we neared the path to the Homestead.

"Can we go by the barn?" I asked.

"Sure," Grandpa replied. He slowed to a crawl, believing I just wanted to look at the barn, and then we'd head home.

"I need to go up to the paddock," I said.

Grandpa stopped, but left the motor running. "Kip, your folks are worried about you."

"Well, you can tell them I'm fine," I said as I got out of the ATV. "I don't want to go home, Grandpa. I want to be alone. And I want to stay here tonight. I need to smell the barn and the hay and the memory of..." I stopped. I couldn't say anymore.

Grandpa nodded. "I understand." He said the words so quietly, I barely heard him. Then he added, "More than you'll ever know, I understand." He rubbed a hand across his chin.

"Will you tell them? Tell them I'm okay, but I want to be alone."

"Yeah." Grandpa nodded again. His eyes ran along the fence line of the paddock, then settled on the barn. "But how about I bring you a sleeping bag? And some food?"

"I'm not hungry."

"A sleeping bag and a thermos of water, then? You'll get a headache if you get dehydrated. Maybe a little bit of fruit? You've had a pretty stressful day, Kip."

"Okay," I said with a shrug. Then I turned away and walked over to the paddock.

I was in the tack room when I heard the ATV coming back from the house. I had decided a sleeping bag would be a nice thing to have if I was going to bunk here overnight on the floor. Maybe I'd sleep in the aisleway so I could look out the doors and see the stars.

Would Liberty look up at the night sky and know I was thinking about him as he saw the same stars? I swallowed the lump in my throat, then went to meet Grandpa.

But it wasn't Grandpa. It was Daddy. My stomach lurched when I saw him.

"Grandpa said you wanted to sleep here tonight."

I crossed my arms over my chest and looked down at the ground.

"I brought you a sleeping bag," he said with a look toward the ATV.

My throat felt tight. I shifted my weight from one leg to the other as my chin began to quiver and my vision blurred with tears.

"And something to eat and drink," Daddy added.

I still couldn't talk. I dropped my arms to my sides, then glanced up at the rafters.

"So, I guess..." he began.

I brought my eyes to Daddy's. We stared at each other for a moment. He took a few steps toward me. I closed the gap and fell into his arms.

"Oh, Daddy," I sobbed. "I'm so sorry."

"Shhh," he said as he smoothed one hand over my hair.

"I don't hate you, Daddy," I cried.

"I know you don't, sweetheart," he whispered.

I hadn't thought there was anything left inside of me that needed to get out until I saw Daddy standing there. The anguish in my heart was nearly unbearable. I put both hands over my face while Daddy held me to his chest, my body wracked with sobs.

"I can't bear to think of Liberty back with that evil man, Daddy. This is killing me."

Daddy rubbed my back. "Shhh," he said again. "I know. I know."

"I said some horrible things to you." The words were muffled by my hands.

"None of that matters." Daddy leaned back and lifted my chin till I was looking him in the eye. "I know what this is doing to you, Kip. Okay? I know."

I took a few deep shuddering breaths.

"We're all upset, honey." He wiped my face. His hand was rough and calloused, but I felt the tenderness. "If there was any way... any way on earth I could fix this... make it right... I would. You know that, don't you?"

"Yes, Daddy," I said, barely more than a whisper.

"You've cried enough today to drown a small village."

A half-hearted laugh escaped my lips.

"And just look what I did to your shirt," I managed to say. Daddy glanced down at the tear stains on his khaki button-down.

"Yikes!" he exclaimed in mock horror.

Another little laugh escaped. Daddy reached over and touched my cheek. We stared at each other for a moment, then I took a step back.

I walked by him to the end of the aisleway, blinking the last of the tears from my eyes. My hair stuck to my damp cheeks, and I ran my fingers through it to get it off my face. I held it in a ponytail on top of my head while I searched my pockets for a hair tie. I didn't have one with me, so let my hair fall back down to my neck.

"Here," Daddy said, reaching for a piece of twine hanging on a nail, the kind used to bind hay bales. He took out his pocketknife and cut off a length of it. "If you're gonna have horses, you better learn all the stuff baling twine is handy for." He nodded toward the top of my head. "Gather it back up and turn around."

I did. Daddy used the twine to secure my hair.

"In the same category as duct tape and WD40?" I asked.

"Far superior," he said. "You'll see."

"And what did you mean by 'if you're gonna have horses?'"

Daddy looked at me for a second or two. Then he took a deep breath. "I think after we've all had some time to recover from this loss, we can talk about getting you a couple of horses."

Funny how the words I'd been waiting my whole life to hear brought no joy whatsoever. I couldn't see beyond the heartbreak of losing Liberty Biscuit. I didn't know if I would ever get over losing him.

All I said was, "A couple?" There wasn't an ounce of enthusiasm in my voice.

"No horse should be alone, Kip."

I nodded. I already knew that, of course. You don't hang around with Grandpa Joe for thirteen-plus years and not gain some commonsense knowledge about horses. It surrounds him like fragrance surrounds a honeysuckle vine.

I looked out at the empty paddock. "The ache of loss is powerful, isn't it, Daddy?"

"There's nothing more powerful than that ache." He walked over to the half-wall of one of the stalls and stacked his hands along the top board, resting his chin on them. He stared out the door overlooking the paddock. "It can make it hard to breathe."

I wasn't sure if Daddy was talking about Grandma Pearl or somebody else. I thought about the photograph in the trunk upstairs.

I stepped beside Daddy and leaned backward against the wall where he was standing, then put a foot up behind me. The sun had fully set. We were surrounded by darkness, except for a small light that burned in the tack room. It leaked its yellow glow into the aisleway, but Daddy's face was in the shadows.

"I never wanted you to feel that ache, Kip. I tried to protect you."

"By not letting me have a pet? That doesn't make any sense, Daddy. You can't protect me from loss. You couldn't protect me from the loss of Grandma Pearl."

"It's more complicated than that."

"How? I don't understand."

He didn't answer me. He just took another great big deep breath. Seemed like both of us were doing a lot of sighing this evening. I let the quiet wrap around us.

Then, the question I'd been afraid to ask came to the surface. "Daddy?" I ventured.

"Hmm." He didn't look over at me. He was still resting his chin on his hands on top of the half-wall, staring out the back door of the stall.

"Who is Henry?"

Daddy stood up straight; his eyes dropped to the ground.

"How do you know about—"

"Up in the loft," I said. "I saw a photograph of you and

another boy on horses. Grandma Pearl's handwriting is on the back. It says: *Charlie and Henry*."

There was a long pause when neither of us spoke. I could hear cicadas in the weeds at the far end of the paddock. Then, "Let's go sit outside," he said.

chapter 9

Daddy walked over to the ATV. He dropped the little tailgate, then spread the sleeping bag out in the bed and climbed up. I followed. We sat with our legs stretched out in front of us and our backs against the frame of the roll bar.

"Henry is my brother."

I was right. My uncle. Why had no one ever talked about him? Daddy tipped his head back to gaze up at the starlit sky and didn't say anything else.

"What happened to him?" I finally asked.

"I guess you're old enough to hear all this," Daddy replied after a moment. He reached out and gave my hand a squeeze, then crossed his arms over his chest like he was cold even though the night was muggy.

"Henry was more than my brother; he was my best friend," he began. "Horses were our life. We rode every day. And you think Grandpa Joe is good with horses? Henry was brilliant. Calm and kind, he could gentle any horse that Grandpa brought home. Even ones who had been so mistreated, you'd think they'd never trust again."

Daddy paused. He shook his head and looked off toward the pasture. The glow of the rising moon defined the fences and cloaked the ground in pewter light. I could see the hint of a smile cross his face as he recalled some moment from his past.

"It was as though Henry and horses spoke the same language," Daddy continued. He uncrossed his arms and dropped his hands down into his lap. He laced and unlaced his fingers.

"I wanted to be like Henry. He was my hero. We always helped Grandpa with all the horses we had at the time, but we each had our own, too. Grandpa bought them for us as yearlings. I named my colt Indigo. Henry named his Padre.

"We weren't allowed to work with our horses the first year we had them. We just let them be...let them be horses. We taught them to accept the halter, we brushed them, trimmed their feet, took care of them. But work them? No. Then Daddy...Grandpa...helped us with groundwork the following year. We weren't allowed to get on their backs till they were four years old.

"One day, Henry and I were here alone. Both horses were coming five—we'd been riding them for about a year. I was showing off, making Indigo rear like the Lone Ranger. Henry kept telling me to knock it off."

Daddy slid off the ATV and took a few steps into the dark. His back was to me.

"But I didn't listen. Henry was carrying two metal buckets, walking past us to go into the barn. I brought Indigo up one last time. I was laughing as Indigo pawed the sky. And then, in the blink of an eye, Henry turned and accidentally dropped one of the buckets. It clattered to the ground, the noise startling Indigo. He hopped forward, still rearing...and...his front hoof...came down on Henry's head."

I gasped, the sound echoing through the night.

Then, silence.

"Why doesn't anyone talk about Henry, Daddy?" I asked after a while. "We talk about Grandma Pearl, keeping her memory alive."

Daddy came back to the ATV and sat beside me.

"Decisions were made during a very traumatic time. Some of them were wrong."

"And this is why you wouldn't let me have a horse." It wasn't a question. I was stating a fact. It made sense to me now.

"I couldn't even stand the smell of them, Kip. Let alone the sight. They just reminded me of the horrible, horrible mistake I made."

It was difficult to imagine how awful the accident must have been for Daddy, and for Grandpa Joe and Grandma Pearl. I could think of no words of comfort.

All I said was, "I'm sorry." I looked down at my hands and shook my head.

"There are parts of that day that never leave my mind, Kip. They haunt every waking moment. The memories invade my sleep."

"How do you survive something like that, Daddy? How do you smile ever again?"

"The old cliché. Time heals. Time heals some of it. And Grandma and Grandpa were pretty amazing. They never blamed me. It was an accident. They tried for years to get me to quit heaping guilt on myself. But how could I *not* blame myself? I don't cope with loss very well."

"What happened to Indigo?" I watched Daddy's face as I said his horse's name. Pain rippled across it.

"I couldn't bear to look at him," he said, staring out at the dark, empty paddock. "It wasn't his fault, but even saying his name made everything too raw. I told Grandpa to get rid of him. I don't know what he did with him, though. If he sold him or...I never asked. And I never touched another horse again."

I knew what he meant about not being able to bear things; I couldn't bear the look on Daddy's face. I blamed myself for asking about Henry and wondered if I would ever learn to keep my mouth shut.

"I'm sorry," I said again.

"Don't be sorry, Kip. It actually feels like a small part of me might heal, now that I've shared this with you."

I wasn't sure I understood, but I nodded. "Do you think Sheriff Ronnie will forgive me for the way I behaved today?" I asked.

"I'm sure he will," Daddy said. "But you can sorta see how a person might say and do things we don't mean when we're upset, can't you?"

I nodded. Then I admitted, "I used to think I had a crush on that lawman."

"Yeah? And what do you think now?"

"Now I think he's the biggest dope on the planet with nary a single redeeming quality."

I didn't turn to see Daddy's face, but I was pretty sure he was smiling. Or trying not to. He said, "You'll have lots of crushes before it's all said and done, Kip. And poor ol' Ronnie was just doing his job. Don't be so hard on him."

"Did you really know Mama was the girl you wanted to marry the second you laid eyes on her?"

"Pretty much."

"Were you worried about her being Black and you being white?"

"Not with Grandma and Grandpa. I knew they'd be accepting."

"What did Grandma Pearl say when she met Mama?"

Daddy laughed at the memory. "Grandma took both Mama's hands and said, 'Look how pretty you are. And you're no bigger than a minute.'"

"That sounds like Grandma Pearl," I said, and smiled. "She and Mama sure loved each other, didn't they?"

"They sure did. Grandpa loves her too."

"Were they against you two marrying, even though they liked Mama?"

"No. But, they had concerns about some of the ignorance we might face."

"What did Grandma Kay and Grandpa Earl say about Mama being with a white boy?"

"They were fine about me being white. But same as Grandma Pearl and Grandpa Joe, they were worried about how others would treat us. They wanted us to move north. They thought we'd have an easier time. But I couldn't leave the farm; didn't want to. And, truthfully, Mama had fallen in love with the farm while we were dating and she loved being in the country. She didn't want to move either."

"Daddy? Are you glad you weren't raised a racist?"

"What a silly question, Kip. Of course, I am."

"Do you think, if Grandma and Grandpa were racists and you were raised that way, that you'd find it within yourself to rise above it?"

"I like to think I would."

"I don't believe we know how to hate when we're born. We learn to hate. Like broccoli."

"Broccoli?" Daddy said, and laughed. "What's broccoli got to do with racism?"

"Well, you know how you hate broccoli?"

"Yeah."

"If you'd never eaten it, ever in your life, you wouldn't know you hated it. Same with people. If some white daddy or some Black daddy never told their white son or Black son to hate the other, they'd never know to do it."

"That's a good way to look at things, but it's a bit more

complicated than that. We're influenced by more than just the way we're raised. Society. Our own community. The way we're treated." Daddy paused. "Why are you asking all these questions about racism?"

"Oh," I said with a big sigh. "I'm just wondering what will happen if I fall in love with a Black boy, but his parents don't like the white side of me. Or if I fall in love with a white boy and his parents don't like the Black side of me."

"Well, I'm sorry you're burdened with these thoughts, Kip. I suppose when the day comes that you fall in love, and he's someone you want to spend the rest of your life with, what his white parents or Black parents think won't really matter."

"It'd be nice for our children to have the kind of grandparents I have."

"Look at the bright side. When you're a grown woman and if the man who falls in love with you happens to have racist parents, well then, you've found a man who is rising above it. Right? He's fallen in love with you regardless of what his parents think or how he was raised."

"That's a good point."

"But none of that really matters."

"Why's that?"

"Cause you're not allowed to date till you're over forty and hopefully racism will have been eradicated from the planet by then."

"Very funny."

"I'll be here all week."

I laughed and shook my head. Then I yawned.

Daddy scooched down, lying flat, then held out his arm. I curled up against him and put my head on his shoulder and yawned again.

"What's wrong with human beings, Daddy?" I asked quietly as I fiddled with his collar. "Why do we hurt each other? Why do we hurt animals?"

"Those are questions for the ages, Kip. I'm not sure anyone could ever answer them." He put his hand on my forehead. I closed my eyes.

"Daddy, I understand why you didn't want me to have a horse. But why didn't you want me to have a cat or a dog?" My eyes were still closed.

"I guess I figured if I let you break me down about a smaller pet, you'd start working on me about a horse. I just couldn't face it, Kip. And your mama knew that. So I put a ban on any pet. I see now it was wrong."

"You can't go through life not loving anything or anyone to avoid getting hurt."

"How'd you get so smart?"

"Must be Mama's side," I said.

Daddy groaned and faked like I'd punched him in the stomach. I laughed.

Then I said, "But I don't feel very smart. If I was smart, Liberty Biscuit would be out there in that paddock right now. Not somewhere scary, wondering what happened...wondering what happened to me."

"What happened today had nothing to do with smarts. Life doesn't always go the way we want it to. Life isn't always fair."

We were both quiet for a minute. Then Daddy took a deep breath.

"Kip?" he said. "I'm gonna tell you something else. Something painful."

"Okay," I said. I thought about sitting up so I could look at his face, but decided to just stay where I was curled against his side.

"When you were about two years old, Mama and I lost a baby."

Now I sat up. The moon cast just enough light for me see Daddy's eyes. He was looking up, into the depths of the stars.

"A little girl," he said. "There were some congenital problems with her heart and lungs. She only lived a few hours...I held her in my arms as she took her final breath."

"Oh, Daddy..." I took his hand.

"We...we named her Elizabeth Grace." Daddy inhaled a deep breath, then slowly let the air back out of his lungs. "It just about did me in. Mama was the strong one. She was so strong. She was the one who got me through it. But...after... later, I said I couldn't face another loss. We didn't try again."

"Daddy," I said.

But he just went on. "I've been a fool," he said. "Mama suffered that horrible loss of Elizabeth. And then she endured the heartbreak of me saying no more children. And then my denying you a pet. A horse, the only thing you wanted in the world. I've been a fool, Kip. And I'm sorry. I'm sorry for what I've denied you. And I'm sorry for what I've denied Mama."

I was still holding Daddy's hand. His left one. I was barely aware of turning his wedding band around and around on his finger. I felt strange, in a way I can't explain. This day was almost turning out to be too much for me. The loss of Liberty and the geldings. Learning about Uncle Henry, and now my baby sister. And Daddy, my strong and perfect daddy who could fix anything, revealing things he didn't have the strength to endure.

It's a scary thing when you realize your daddy has flaws and weaknesses—when you realize your daddy is human.

"Daddy," I repeated.

"Hmm?"

"I love you." I put my head back down on his shoulder and closed my eyes again.

"I love you, too, Kip. More than you'll ever know."

chapter 10

"Mama!" I hollered. "Mama! Where are you?"

"Upstairs," Mama answered.

I raced for the stairs and took them two at a time.

"What's wrong?" Mama said, coming out of her bedroom, a look of concern on her face.

"I need you to take me into town," I replied, breathless, but not from running up the stairs. I was breathless over an idea I had. "If you can't take me," I said, rushing on, "I'll walk."

I already knew Daddy or Grandpa Joe couldn't take me; they were busy in the orchards.

"Slow down," Mama said. "Why do you need to go into town?"

I took Mama's hand and gave it a squeeze. "Oh, Mama! Why didn't we think of this!" I turned and ran back down the stairs. "C'mon!"

Mama stood motionless at the top of the stairs. "Think of what, Katherine Pearl? You tell me what's going on."

"I'll tell you on the way to town." I rushed out the door, calling, "Hurry, Mama!" over my shoulder.

Several weeks had gone by since Liberty Biscuit and the geldings had been returned to Len Parker. I pined for them, especially Liberty, just as badly as the day they were taken from our farm. It was almost September. My fourteenth birthday was coming up. Daddy told me I could start looking for two horses to bring home. He even told Aunt Betty and Uncle Dale to let us know if they heard of any who might be a good match for our family.

But—are you ready for this?—I declined. I told Daddy I couldn't face it. I had promised Liberty Biscuit I would do anything and everything in my power to get him back. It had become all I could think about.

I had asked Sheriff Ronnie to tell that creep Len Parker we wanted to buy Liberty and the geldings. Len Parker refused to sell.

Short of stealing Liberty like a thief in the night, I couldn't figure out a way to keep my promise to him. But I wasn't willing to give up. I wasn't sure I would ever give up. There had to be some way to bring him home where he belonged.

The answer was right under my nose. I had been sitting alone in the nook of the kitchen, staring into the woods. My knees were drawn up to my chin. I was sorta rocking back and forth, lost in thought, when it crossed my mind to go for a walk. I needed to feed my crows. They still hadn't brought me a present. But that didn't matter.

Then maybe I'd continue on to my not-so-secret spot down by the creek.

I stretched my legs out along the window seat and leaned forward, my right hand resting on the sill. Absentmindedly, I ran my fingers along the smooth wood. That's when I felt the indentations from Liberty's teeth marks where he'd bit the sill the day Mama fed him apple slices through the window.

A sad laugh escaped my throat.

"You little hooligan," I said aloud. "You were worth all the mischief you got into, and every sore muscle we got from fixing fences, and every penny we spent taking care of you."

That's when it hit me. I sat up straight as an arrow. I looked down at Liberty's teeth marks, then out to where Sheriff Ronnie had been standing the day he told us the judge reinstated custody of Liberty and the geldings back to Len Parker *after he reimbursed the county for the vet bills and the feed and hay they'd consumed while they were at the fairgrounds.*

I nearly stumbled over my own feet getting out of the window seat. I ran to the phone and dialed the sheriff's office. I asked the woman who answered if I could speak to Sheriff Ronnie. She asked for my name. I didn't say, "Kip." I told her, "Katherine Pearl Baker," and I added that it was an emergency.

Which, it turned out, was not a wise thing to say to a law enforcement official when you don't have an actual emergency. She started asking all sorts of questions, wanting to know if I was in danger, if someone was injured, and did I need 911. I rushed to assure her I was fine, admitting I didn't have an *actual* emergency.

"What's wrong, Kip?" Sheriff Ronnie said when he came to the phone.

"Everything is *right*," I said. "I'm calling to ask if you'd give me ten minutes of your time. That is, if I can get Mama to drive me into town. I haven't asked her yet."

"Ms. Shirley here says *you said* you had an emergency."

"No, sir. I do not. Not *really*. I just want—"

"She said you were talking a mile a minute and sounded like you were gonna come out of your skin."

"Yes, sir. That part is true."

"But there's nothing wrong?"

"Yes, sir. I mean, no, sir, nothing is wrong."

"Your mama and daddy okay? Your grandpa?"

"Yes, sir."

I was inwardly rolling my eyes over all the "yes, sirs" and "no, sirs." But the self-inflicted word of the day was *contrite.* Thankfully, Sheriff Ronnie and I were talking on the phone, and he couldn't see my expression.

"So, why do you need to see me?"

"I'd rather tell you in person. Sir."

"And everything out there at your place is fine?"

Yes! I wanted to scream. Ms. Shirley hit the nail on the head when she said I was about to come out of my skin. But I calmly replied, "Yes, sir."

I heard him sigh. "Alright. You get your mama to bring you in here before noon. I'll be in my office."

"Yes, sir! Thank you, sir!"

"Kip?"

"Yes, sir?"

"Knock it off with the 'sirs.'"

"Yes, sir."

That's when I hung up and went hollering for Mama.

chapter 11

I was hopping up and down beside Mama's car when she came out of the house.

"You better start talking," she said as she went to the driver's side.

A half-hour later, Mama pulled into the parking lot of the sheriff's office but didn't shut the engine off.

"Aren't you coming in?" I asked.

"Nope," she replied. "I'll be across the street at the bookstore. You come get me when you're done. I believe you've got this, Katherine Pearl. You didn't let the heartbreak defeat you. You stayed strong and reasoned out a viable argument for getting Liberty and those geldings back where they belong. With us."

I put my hand on the door handle. "Thank you, Mama."

Before I got out, Mama reached over and gave my arm a squeeze. She smiled and said, "I'm proud of you, my child."

I nodded and swallowed the lump in my throat.

"Have a seat, Kip," Sheriff Ronnie said from behind his desk.

I sat.

He closed a folder and set it aside, then steepled his hands in front of his face.

"What's so important that you needed to see me in person?" he asked.

I took a deep breath. If this didn't work, I wasn't sure I would ever get Liberty and the horses back. It had to work. Otherwise, all I had was my original plan A . . . which involved stealing them like a thief in the night. Which I knew very well wasn't really a plan at all. Nor was it one I had the wherewithal or the courage to execute.

I scooted forward to the edge of the chair.

"Sheriff Ronnie," I began, wishing to evoke the seriousness of what I was about to say. "May I ask what the purpose was of requiring Mr. Parker to reimburse the county for feed and hay and the care his animals received while they were impounded at the fairgrounds?"

Sheriff Ronnie pursed his lips and blinked a few times. "Well, Mr. Parker's neglect of the animals was irresponsible. The fact that the county had to intervene on behalf of his animals does not warrant a depletion in our limited funding. The county had just cause to require reimbursement as part of the punishment."

I nodded and looked down at the floor. I focused on a chip in one of the squares of faded linoleum tile while I tried to slow my breathing.

"Sheriff Ronnie," I said, bringing my eyes back up to his. "The Baker family cared for one white donkey for nearly six weeks and two geldings for one full month at their farm. They were given excellent and commendable care according to Samantha Caldwell, DVM (that stands for 'doctor of veterinary medicine'). The care those animals received does not warrant a depletion in the Baker family's limited funding. It would be, in my opinion, fair and reasonable to expect reimbursement. If Mr. Parker is unable to reimburse the Baker family for the amount spent on his animals' care, one white donkey and two geldings should be returned to KPB Stables in place of payment."

Sheriff Ronnie stared at me for a moment without saying a word. And then he laughed. Sort of. It was more like a humorless puff of air.

"Huh."

He stood up and crossed his arms over his chest. I felt a sinking weight in the pit of my stomach. He narrowed his eyes and continued to stare at me.

I bit the inside of my mouth, but my eyes never wavered from his.

"I'll be damned," he finally said as he dropped his arms to his sides. "Why didn't any of us think of this before? Including Judge Andrews. Judge Andrews should have thought of this." He shook his head and ran a hand through his hair. "*I* should have thought of this." He shook his head once more and again said, "Huh." And then, "You're a genius, Kip."

"Well..." I stuck a toe into that chip in the linoleum tile.

"KPB Stables? What's that?" the sheriff asked.

"Katherine Pearl Baker," I said.

"Did you just make that up?"

"Yep." I smiled. Then my expression got serious again. "Do you think we got a shot at this?"

"I do," Sheriff Ronnie said. "I want you to go home and sit down with your Grandpa Joe. You two figure out everything you put into caring for Parker's animals. Don't forget anything. Feed, hay, medicine...even fuel running back and forth in the ATV. And it would be great if you had receipts. Did you all save receipts?"

I gave him a sideways glance that silently said, *Seriously?*

He laughed and said, "Oh, I forgot who your mama is for a minute. CPAs sure are serious about receipts, aren't they?"

"They sure are." I got up to leave. "Thank you, Ronnie." I used his first name only, elevating him back to the status of family friend.

He gave me a smile, and I turned toward the door.

"Kip," he said, stopping me. "Don't forget your time. Your time has value. You add that in, for both you and your grandpa. Plus a flat fee for boarding three animals for a month."

"Okay." I started backing out of his office. I was eager to go find Mama and get back home to tell Grandpa Joe.

"Also," he said, then shifted his eyes toward the door. "You didn't hear this from me, but the amount Parker owes you has the potential to be hefty. You get what I'm saying?"

"I think so."

"Don't leave anything out."

"We won't."

chapter 12

*T*he phone rang, startling me. I was sitting in the nook of our kitchen, reading, and I was home alone. Mama and Daddy had taken Grandpa Joe to Savannah. He was finally having that bad knee replaced. He'd made plans to stay with close friends in the city for the pre-operative testing, and his friends would also drive him to the hospital on the day of the surgery so Mama and Daddy could return home to the farm.

They'd wanted me to join them for the drive, but I'd declined after learning that Mama planned on hitting the mall. *No thanks.*

"You sure, Kip?" Daddy had asked.

He'd hoped I'd come along so he didn't have to endure the mall on his own while

Mama shopped. I'd tried not to laugh at the desperate look on his face and the pleading tone of his voice.

"I'm sure," I'd responded and then hugged Grandpa goodbye.

As the three of them headed out the door, I'd called to Daddy. When he turned around, I gave him a thumbs up and mouthed, "You got this." He just shook his head and rolled his eyes.

"Baker residence," I said when I picked up the phone. Mama and Daddy had been gone for about an hour. I figured they'd just be getting into Savannah.

"Kip? It's Sheriff Ronnie. Go put fresh water in your horse troughs. Len Parker has relinquished custody of his animals. They're legally yours."

"What?" was all I managed to say.

"You heard me." There was a smile in his tone of voice.

"Lib...Liberty, too?"

"Liberty, too."

I couldn't take it. I slid right down the cabinet like spilled milk and sat on the floor. "I don't know what to say," I gasped. "I don't believe it."

"Believe it. But we need to expedite this exchange. Today. I'm bringing them out to your place in an hour."

"An hour?" I looked at the clock. It wasn't quite noon. Mama and Daddy wouldn't be home till after four o'clock or later.

"Is there a problem?"

"No," I said. "I...I just can't believe it."

"You did a good job, Kip. You put together a professional but fair presentation for the judge. I felt certain he'd rule in your favor. Parker didn't even try to fight it or ask for time to come up with the funds for your reimbursement. And..." He paused. "I don't want to upset you, but when I pulled into his place to present the paperwork, I caught him hitting the black horse across the face with a crop."

"Oh, no." I winced. I squeezed my eyes shut to try to block the picture from my head.

"He's been rearrested, fined, and banned from owning animals for five years."

"Just five years?"

"It's the way it is here, Kip. When you're of voting age you can work on getting the laws related to animal cruelty changed. But with my having witnessed an act of abuse, coupled with your demand for compensation, he didn't have a chance. He knew it. The two horses and one mischievous white donkey now belong to KPB Stables."

"Thank you, Ronnie. Thank you, so much." Emotions were taking over and I swallowed hard. "I...I guess I'll see you when you get here."

"Well, actually, it's not me bringing them. I can't get away. And I can't spare a deputy right now. I asked one of my auxiliary guys to haul them. He's new to the area. A young man named Jason. He's using my truck and trailer, and he doesn't know anything about horses. Your daddy or grandpa will have to handle things. Okay?"

"Okay." The word just came out. I knew it was wrong not to tell the sheriff I was home alone. But I didn't want to risk him putting off bringing my Liberty home. And I didn't want Liberty or the geldings to spend one more minute with that evil man, Len Parker.

It was like the day they were taken from me. I stood in front of the barn, crying as the sound of the clanking trailer and Liberty's screeching bray reverberated through the woods. But today, I wasn't crying because I was distraught. I was crying and smiling because that beautiful, wonderful, magnificent sound was coming *toward* me.

When Sheriff Ronnie's truck and trailer came into view, I glanced at the face of the young man driving. He looked white as a ghost. Which wouldn't be so bad except for the fact that he was Black. I wondered what was wrong and worried something may have happened to one of the horses or Liberty.

When he came to a stop, I ran right past him to the back of the trailer. I couldn't stop and offer the guy a proper greeting. I couldn't help myself.

I jumped up on the fender of the trailer. All three were on their feet and appeared fine. Liberty had stopped braying and came to nuzzle me through the slats.

"Oh, my Liberty!" I cried out as I touched his face. "You're home. You're home." I blinked the tears from my eyes.

The young man had gotten out of the truck and was using the sleeve of his auxiliary uniform shirt to wipe the sweat off his face. He appeared slightly out of breath. I wondered what in the world was wrong.

"Are you okay?" I asked, walking back up to the truck. "You look sick."

"I've never pulled a trailer before," he replied, looking off across the pasture. "I was a wreck." He shook his head and took a deep breath. "Being responsible for their lives? Man, that's some nerve-wracking stuff, right there."

While it was commendable that he cared about his precious cargo, I looked at him with the sympathy one might offer a kitten in the rain.

"Well, you poor thing," I said.

"I'll be alright," he said. "In a year or two. And maybe after some intense therapy." His hair was unfashionably long. Most of the boys I knew kept their hair cropped close to their heads. But, somehow, the halo of an afro worked on this boy.

"Do you need some water?" I asked.

"No, I'm alright," he repeated. He turned to look at me for the first time. He stared for a moment, then asked, "But what's wrong with *you*? Why're you crying?"

"I'm not crying," I said. "I just have tears in my eyes 'cause I'm happy."

"What is it with women? Cry when they're happy. Cry when they're sad." He was wearing a lopsided grin. "Never heard of such a thing," he added.

There was a good chance, based on his teasing tone of voice, he was throwing down the gauntlet for a bout of bantering. I accepted the challenge while trying to ignore the fact that he'd referred to me as a woman.

"Yeah, well," I said with a fake frown. "I've never heard of a boy who didn't know how to pull a trailer."

"Well, you've heard of one now." Then he put his hand up to the side of his mouth and whispered, "And I'd be obliged if you didn't tell Sheriff Alton that I looked like I was going to lose my lunch when I pulled in here."

"Deal," I said.

He reached out to shake my hand. "I'm Jason. Jason Starr with two Rs."

"Nice to meet you, Jason Starr with two Rs," I said, putting my hand in his. "I'm Kip. Katherine. Or Kip. Whatever."

He smiled. "It's nice to meet you, Kip-Katherine."

I felt my cheeks get hot.

Jason didn't seem to notice as he looked around. "Sheriff Alton said your daddy or your grandpa would be here to help unload them."

"Yeah," I said. "About that. They got tied up and busy with a few things. So, it's just me and you."

"Oh, no," Jason said. Then he put both hands up like Diana Ross and The Supremes singing, *"Stop, in the name of love."* "I ain't touching no two-thousand-pound horse. I'm a city boy, through and through."

"Well, first of all," I said. "Horses don't weigh two thousand pounds. At least, these horses don't. Some breeds of draft do, but not these guys. These guys only weigh about eight or nine hundred pounds, and they need to gain about a hundred more."

I suddenly wondered why I was being so chatty. I wondered if it was because I thought Jason was cute.

"And second of all," I continued. "You don't have to touch them. All you have to do is back the trailer up to the aisleway of the barn. I'll handle the rest."

But Jason was already shaking his head.

"What's wrong?" I asked.

"Did you not hear me a minute ago? I've never pulled a trailer before. Where do you think I acquired the skills to *back* one?"

I looked from Jason to the barn, then back to Jason. Now I wasn't sure what to do. I hadn't considered the contingency of inept trailering skills.

"Why can't you just lead them off?" Jason asked.

I looked over at the horses. They weren't wearing halters.

"How did you get them in the trailer?" I asked, ignoring Jason's question.

"I didn't. That Len Parker guy loaded them, then he took their halters off, saying he wasn't giving away any of his tack."

I knew I could just let Liberty out and he'd stay right with me in the yard. But the geldings might run off. I could try to halter them, I supposed, but they appeared nervous and were jigging back and forth. I decided it might be dangerous trying to halter them in the confines of the trailer.

I was probably already going to catch what-for because I'd failed to tell Ronnie I was here alone. It would be a million times worse if I got hurt. But I needed to make a decision. Soon. The horses were getting more and more agitated.

"I need to let them out in a fenced area," I said, looking from the paddocks to the pasture.

"Well, there needs to be enough room for me to just pull in a big, wide circle," Jason said. "No backing involved."

It would have to be the fifty-acre field. It was our only choice.

Jason pulled through the gate and drove into the pasture. I closed the gate behind him and made sure it was latched. We met up at the back of the trailer.

"Let's each open one door, at the same time," I said. "They're gonna rush out, so move quick and stand near the side of the trailer."

When the geldings jumped out, I saw that there was a rope around the black's neck. I hadn't noticed it looking through the slats of the trailer.

"Oh, no," I groaned as they ran in a pounding gallop to a far corner.

"What's wrong?" Jason asked.

"That rope," I said, and pointed in the direction the horses had run. "I didn't notice it. You can't turn a horse out with a rope around his neck. It's dangerous."

Liberty was hopping around and bucking, then he came to rest his head against my chest.

"You're home, my Liberty Biscuit," I said, hugging him to me. My happiness over having him back temporarily overshadowed my concern about that rope. But only for a moment.

I sighed as I watched the geldings settle down and move off to graze. "What am I going to do?"

"I hope that's a rhetorical question, 'cause I don't have a clue what you're gonna do."

I looked over at Jason and smiled, despite my worry. I liked the fact that he'd used the word *rhetorical*. Me and words. I wondered if that was going to be the way some boy would win my heart someday—with a great big, bright, shiny vocabulary.

"How old are you?" I asked him.

"Seventeen. Why?"

"Just wondering. You don't look old enough to be on Sheriff Alton's auxiliary. I thought you had to be twenty."

"Nope, you just have to've graduated from high school."

"And you have? Already?" I asked with raised eyebrows.

"Yep," Jason said. "I took accelerated classes and graduated a year early. I got big plans for college."

"Wow," I said. "Good for you. What do you want to be?"

"A veterinarian," he said. Then he pointed to the horses while vigorously shaking his head and quickly added, "Small animals! Very, very small animals."

I laughed.

Jason crossed his arms over his chest. "Do you need anything else? Anything that doesn't involve getting ropes off the necks of horses."

"Yeah," I said. "I do need something. If you've got time. There's no water for the horses over here. Would you help me carry a trough from the paddock? Then I'll string a few hoses together."

"Sure," Jason agreed.

We started walking toward the barn. Liberty bounded along with us. I opened the gate and Liberty tried to squeeze through, brushing against Jason and knocking him one step sideways. Jason let out a high-pitched squeal and jumped up on the rail of the fence.

"That animal is crazy!" he cried.

Jason's chocolate-drop eyes were rimmed in white. I had never seen, or heard, anything so hilarious in my life. I doubled over with laughter.

"What are you laughing about? He tried to kill me."

"No, he didn't," I said, still laughing. "He's a lamb. Get down."

"Move him away. Then I'll get down."

"C'mon, Liberty," I said, luring my sweet donkey back into the pasture. He trotted off to join the geldings.

Jason and I each took an end of a long metal trough from the paddock and carried it out to the pasture. We linked two hoses together, then stood watching the three graze as the trough filled with water.

"It's nice out here," Jason said, looking around. "Peaceful."

"Are you from here in Georgia?" I asked.

"Nope," Jason said. "I was born and raised in Atlanta."

I looked at him like he had two heads. "Newsflash," I said. "Atlanta is *in* Georgia."

Jason winked and gave me a quick smile. "You said *here* in Georgia. Atlanta is a different world compared to here."

"That sure is the truth," I said. I'd only been to Atlanta a few times. He was right about it being a different world. Even Savannah couldn't be put in the same category as Atlanta. "Speaking of here, if you're off to college, what are you doing in our little town?"

"My grandparents live here. I'm going to spend a year or so going to school in Savannah. Get my feet wet for college life, so to speak. Then I'll apply to UGA in Athens or Auburn in Alabama."

"Don't they have colleges in Atlanta?"

"Sure they do. But I'll have you know I'm the kind of person who takes a bite out of life. I spent seventeen years in the city. I wanted to experience a bit of rural living." Jason's head was high and his eyes were shining. "Plus," he added, "I miss my grammy. She spoils me."

I smiled, getting the distinct feeling there was something very special about this boy. "Why'd you join the sheriff auxiliary?" I asked.

Jason shrugged. "I moved here at the beginning of the summer. I wanted to stay busy. Get involved in the community." Then he looked over at me. "So what about you, Kip-Katherine? What're your big plans?"

Now I shrugged. "I don't really have any. Yet. I'm only fourteen. Or I will be soon."

"Fourteen?" Jason asked with a look of surprise on his face. "I pegged you a little older than that."

"I'm tall for my age. Already taller than my mama."

"Not just that," he said. "The way you talk. The way you carry yourself."

"Hmm," I said. I found it interesting that he'd noticed such things. Then I added, "Mama and Daddy say I have an old soul."

"Well, your soul may be old, but your face sure is pretty. I don't think I've ever seen eyes such an unusual color of green. They're mesmerizing, sitting there against your dark skin."

Jason was staring at me. I suddenly felt bashful and looked away.

"They're like the scales on a mermaid," he said. But now his tone of voice was completely different than it had been when he was talking about my eyes—he was back to bantering.

I laughed as my feelings of shyness evaporated and his playful, lopsided grin reappeared.

"Mermaid scales!" I scoffed. "How would you know what their scales look like? You have any personal friends who are mermaids?"

"More like casual acquaintances."

We were both smiling. Just then the water trough began to overflow, and I rushed to turn the spigot off.

"Well, I guess I better get back to town," Jason said.

"Okay," I said. I went to open the gate for him while he circled the truck and trailer around in the pasture.

Before he drove through the gate, he said, "Can I ask you something?"

"Sure."

"Is one of your parents white?"

"Can I ask you something?" I shot back. "Why didn't you ask me if one of my parents is Black?"

Jason shrugged. "I dunno. I guess 'cause I'm Black. And Black is normal to me. If I was white I probably would've asked if one of your parents was Black."

"Normal?" I asked. "So everyone different than you is *abnormal*?"

"Touché," Jason said with a little laugh. "How about *familiar*? That a better word?"

"That's better," I said more softly. "My daddy is white." I paused, then, "Does that bother you?"

"Doesn't bother me. It's just not something I've seen around here very often. It's fairly common in Atlanta. But . . . small towns? I was just curious."

It was only recently that I'd been pondering my racial status. I tried to think if I knew any other kid like me. The only ones who came to mind were a brother and sister whose mother was white and father was Asian. I couldn't be the only kid in our small town with one Black parent and one white parent. Could I?

The green welcome sign at our town border said: Population 6378. That same number had been on the sign for as long as I could remember. I guess no one wanted to get out the paint and update it every time someone was born or died. But I couldn't tell you what the Black-to-white ratio was. It seemed to me the population leaned toward mostly Black. I had never felt as though anyone looked down on me because my daddy was white.

Maybe it was because the Bakers were a longstanding and respected part of the community. I thought about the fact that Daddy rarely went into town. And Mama and Daddy hardly ever went into town together. When Mama could get Daddy to leave the farm, she preferred to go all the way over to Savannah for the bigger stores. I wondered if there were people, Black or white, who disapproved of their marriage. Which would mean they disapproved of me.

Jason lifted his hand. "It was nice to meet you, Kip-Katherine. See ya 'round."

I waved back. "See ya, Jason Starr—with two Rs."

chapter 13

" Mama, how am I gonna get that rope off his neck?"

She and I were at the Homestead, watching Liberty and the geldings graze in the large pasture. They'd been back on our farm for nearly a week.

Both Mama and Daddy had been seriously upset that I hadn't let Sheriff Ronnie know I was alone when he'd called to tell me the good news about Len Parker relinquishing ownership. The idea of me handling the horses without Grandpa had scared them both into fits. But when I told them how I'd had Jason just drive into the pasture so we hadn't had to handle them at all, they'd been somewhat placated. I didn't tell them the real reason was because Jason didn't know how to back up the trailer.

I'd been trying to entice the black horse into a stall with grain and apples so I could slip the rope off his neck, but he wasn't having any of it. Whatever that creep Len Parker had done to him since we'd had him last had put us back to square one in terms of trust. Who could blame him?

The bay would come into the barn, but not the black. And when he was loose in the pasture? I couldn't get within thirty feet of him.

Grandpa's knee surgery had gone well, but he was still in Savannah, staying with his friends while he healed. He had been thrilled when I called to tell him Liberty and the geldings had been returned to us. But he was as upset as I was when he learned about the rope on the black horse. We were both concerned he'd get it caught on something and possibly hang himself.

"Giving a horse the time he needs is always the best technique, Kip," Grandpa said when we talked on the phone. "But this is a serious situation. I'm not sure what to tell you. Have you asked Uncle Dale or Aunt Betty if they could come help?"

"They're on vacation. Up to the mountains with Fancy and Prism."

"Hmm," Grandpa said, thinking.

"When are you coming home?" I asked.

"Not for another week," he said. "But I'll still need to take it easy. Have you asked your daddy to help?"

"Yes," I replied shortly. "He says he's too busy."

"Don't fault him, Kip," Grandpa said. "The trauma of that day has him in an unrelenting grip. I don't know if he'll ever be able to work with any horse, ever again."

Grandpa knew that Daddy had told me about Henry. I felt bad I didn't know about this uncle of mine when Grandma Pearl was alive. I would've hugged her tight and told her how sorry I was that she lost her boy. I also wished I'd known because it explained why Daddy had always been so against having horses. Before I knew the whole story, it all just seemed so unreasonable and strange. But now, knowing what happened, it all made sense.

Well, not all of it. I still didn't understand why no one spoke of Henry. Daddy had just said, "Decisions were made, and some of them weren't right," but it still didn't make a lick of sense to me. It made me feel sad, thinking about Henry's memory banished to an old trunk in the loft of the barn.

While Grandpa was in Savannah, Mama had been coming to tend the horses with me in the mornings. Liberty was always so happy to see us both. I do believe that donkey got more hugs and kisses than any donkey on the planet.

We slipped a halter on the bay a few times and I held him so Mama could brush him. She told me she hadn't realize that horses smelled so heavenly. She also said she found the chores of caring for them pleasant and relaxing. She especially enjoyed sweeping the aisleway of the barn.

After chores, we'd stand by the pasture fence together, watching the horses and their donkey companion move about the field.

"I've got to figure out how to get that rope off his neck," I told Mama. "There has to be some way to safely do this." I gazed across the pasture. "Some way..."

Mama put both elbows up across the top rail of the fence. "I wish there was something I could do to help," she said. "But I don't know a thing about horses."

"I won't be able to live with myself if something happens to him," I said quietly. "After everything these horses have been through. To finally be with people who love them. But now that dang rope. I gotta figure this out, Mama."

Mama nodded her head in agreement. Then, slowly, she stood up straight and dropped her hands to her sides. There was an odd expression on her face as she looked beyond the horses, into the woods.

"What is it, Mama?"

"Maybe...maybe there *is* a way I can help," she said.

"How?" I asked.

"Katherine Pearl," she said. "I'm going to tell you something." She paused and took a deep breath. Then she began again in a firmer voice, as though she'd made a decision. "I'm going to tell you something that may come as a bit of a shock. Maybe even a big shock."

"Okay," I said. Her tone of voice made me jittery.

"Well, not *maybe* a big shock. It will *definitely* be a big shock."

"Um, okay," I repeated. "I guess." My stomach did a little flip. I wasn't sure if I was up for a big shock.

We stared at each other for a moment, then Mama said, "I know someone who can get that rope off his neck."

"You do?"

Mama put her hands on her hips. "I do." But then she took another deep breath.

"Who?" I asked. I didn't understand why she was behaving so oddly.

"First, you have to make me a promise. Will you promise me something, Kip?"

I crinkled my brow in a worried way as I said, "Yes, Mama."

"You have to promise me you won't tell anyone how you found out about this."

"Found out about what?"

"I'm not asking you to lie. Do you understand me? I would never ask you to lie. But for now, you need to leave me out of it."

"Out of what?"

"If Daddy and everybody else find out I told you, it'll just make things worse. And trust me, once everybody knows that *you* know, things are going to get worse before they get better. They just don't need to know I told you. Yet. But I guarantee you, once this is all out and everybody settles down, things *will* get better. And I will admit to your father that I told you. After...But right now, it's time for this foolishness to end."

"Mama, you're not making any sense." I blinked my eyes at her as I took a few steps back.

Mama reached for my hand and pulled me close.

"Katherine Pearl...your Uncle Henry isn't dead."

My mouth dropped open, but no words came out.

"Your Uncle Henry isn't dead," Mama repeated.

"I...what are...I don't..."

"And he can help you with that horse," she added, ignoring my stammering.

"Does Daddy know he's alive?"

Mama smiled. "Of course he knows."

Now, all of this made absolutely no sense. None. And I said so to Mama. "If Uncle Henry didn't die the day of that accident with Daddy's horse, then why all the grief? Mama! What the heck is going on?"

"Let's go sit down," Mama said.

We walked back to the barn and sat on some hay bales in the aisleway. Mama leaned forward with her arms on her knees and clasped her hands together as she contemplated the floor. I reasoned she was thinking about the best way to say whatever it was she was about to tell me.

Mama sighed, and then said, "Henry is terribly disfigured."

"In what way?"

"That day when Indigo reared, his hoof came down on Henry and scraped the entire right side of his face, down to the bone."

I gasped and put a hand over my mouth.

"Henry was knocked unconscious. They rushed him to the trauma center in Savannah. Once he was stabilized, he was taken to surgery, but he lost his right eye, his right ear, part of his jaw.... His right shoulder was also damaged and his right leg. His hip. The full force of Indigo's weight had come down on him."

"Oh, Mama," I said, shaking my head.

"I know this is difficult to hear." She rubbed her hands together as though they were cold.

"Where is Henry now? Where does he live?" I pictured him alone in a nursing home or some special place where he received full-time care.

Mama lifted her eyes, then shifted them to the open cross-buck doors and the woods beyond. "Right back there," she said.

"Henry was only twenty years old when this happened," Mama began. "He had his whole life in front of him. But once he got out of the hospital, and after he'd endured months of surgeries, he sank into a terrible depression. His face was disfigured. His right arm was nearly useless. And he walked with a painful limp. I wasn't part of this family yet, but Grandma Pearl told me about holding him and trying to comfort him as he sobbed, as he cried that his life was over. He felt no one could bear to look at him. That no one would ever want him. That he'd never know love or marriage or have children."

I felt tears stinging my eyes. I didn't know what to say. I could see Mama was upset, retelling all this.

She looked over at me. "It was awful, Katherine, seeing Grandma Pearl's broken heart and imagining what Henry had gone through."

"I can't...I can't even imagine, Mama."

"They worried Henry was going to take his own life. He even said he wished he'd died that day of the accident, rather than suffer the injuries. But, after a lot of pleading, talking, and a lot more tears, Henry promised Grandma Pearl that he would try to create a life for himself if they would allow him to do it as a recluse."

"What do you mean?"

"As far as the community and anyone who had known Henry—his friends, family—were concerned, he wanted to be 'dead.' He agreed to maintain contact, but only if he never had to face another human being for the rest of his life. He told Grandma to take down any photos of him from before the accident. Pack his life away. And never talk about him to anyone, ever again. The family agreed, just to keep him alive."

"So...he just lives in the woods?"

"Well, he has a home," Mama replied slowly. "Grandpa gave him the fifty acres that backs up to this property. He and Henry dismantled the original house from the Homestead and used the lumber to build Henry a small cottage."

"What does he do all day?"

"He gardens. Grows most of his own food, and puts a lot of it up in preserves. You should see his root cellar. He loves to read, and he does some writing. He's also been adding on to his barn."

"A barn? Why does he need a barn?"

"He has horses."

"What?" I cried. Mama said those words like she was just chatting about the weather. I couldn't believe it. "You mean to tell me there have been horses right here on our land my entire life and I never knew about it?"

"Yes," Mama said without looking at me. "And he can help you get that rope off the black's neck. He's a brilliant horseman."

"And I've had an uncle, right here, who could have been my friend? Someone to do things with? Someone who shares my love of horses?"

Mama nodded slowly.

"Good grief! This family needs a serious adjustment."

"I agree with you, Kip. Like I said, it's time for this foolishness to end. And I believe you're the one to effect the change. That's why I'm telling you all this."

"I thought all that land back there belonged to the timber company."

"No, it looks like it's part of the timber land, because of the planted pines. Grandpa did that on purpose so folks wouldn't notice Henry's house back there. They also planted a thick row of cedars. Unless someone knows his place is back there, it's unlikely you would ever find it. The only clear way to his house is through our land."

"So that path...through the woods there," I said, pointing behind the barn. "That leads to his house?"

Mama nodded again.

"I noticed it one day when Grandpa Joe and I were checking the fence lines. I even said something. Grandpa just shrugged it off as a deer trail." I thought for a minute, then asked, "Have you met him, Mama?"

"Yes," she said. "He refused to meet me when Daddy and I were just dating, but after we married and I was living here on the farm, Henry finally agreed to an introduction."

"Was it hard? I mean...to look at him?"

"In some ways, it was. Yes. At first. But I'll tell you something else. After I got to know him and we became friends, and he let his guard down and let me see his personality...I no longer saw the scars." Mama smiled. "I just see a kind and gentle man."

"Did he used come up to the house? To be with the family? Eat supper with you all?"

"No." Mama shook her head. "Not to eat with the family. He really keeps to himself. I only see him six or seven times a year. It's what he prefers, and I respect that. We've kind of worked out a system, he and I. I bring him books, we talk about this and that, and when I get ready to leave, he says something like, 'Maybe I'll see you on the second Saturday in May, Elise.' That might be two months away, or it might be a couple weeks away, but that's when I go back for a visit. Whatever day he mentioned."

"What about Daddy and Uncle Henry? Do they talk?"

"They do. But rarely. There's a strain between them. Even after all this time. Daddy still struggles with guilt. And he never agreed with the idea of Henry living alone, sequestered away in the woods. Daddy won't go to Henry's house. He feels Henry should be living with the family. Helping with the farm. Socializing. But that wasn't Daddy's decision to make."

"I think I agree with Daddy." I got to my feet and went to look out the doors, in the general direction of Henry's house. "How can someone live so isolated?"

"Well, we all agree it's no way to live," Mama said. "But..." She shrugged. "What can we do? Except respect Henry's wishes. When Grandma Pearl was alive, she saw him the most. Every week, at least. She was his connection to life."

"He must be terribly lonely since Grandma Pearl died."

I wondered if Henry had ever seen me. Did he hear Liberty braying every morning? Did he know there were horses at the Homestead?

I asked Mama, "Does he know who I am?"

"Yes, Kip. Henry knows who you are. He and Grandpa used to meet up here at the barn—but that stopped this summer when you started hanging around here all day, every day. So Grandpa goes to his house now. Or they meet at the river and fish. He's always asked about you. He loved hearing about when you first walked. Your first words. And I know both Grandma and Grandpa talked to him about your love of horses."

I had to think about that for a minute. I sat back down on the hay bale. Here was someone I never even met, who was interested in hearing about how I was growing up?

"He cared about me?" I asked.

"He *cares* about you. You're his niece. He held you . . . when you were an infant. He was in awe of your tiny little hands." Mama smiled at the memory. "You were about a year old the last time I took you to see him. I wanted you to know him. But..."

"But what?"

"He was worried you'd be afraid of him. As you got older. He insisted I stop bringing you to visit while you were still too young to react to his scars. He didn't want you to know anything about him."

"So, all these years, I could've had a friend?" I repeated. "Someone who shares my love of horses, besides Grandpa?"

I felt something stirring inside me. Deep down inside me. And I'll tell you what that something was. It was anger. Anger that my family would deny me the love of my uncle. Anger at my uncle for denying himself the love and companionship of his family and friends.

I stood up, in an abrupt way meant to reveal how angry I was.

"Mama," I said. "I'll see you later."

"Where are you going?"

"To meet my Uncle Henry."

"Kip, wait a minute," Mama said, reaching out to stop me. I turned to her.

"We need to think about this," she said. "This is going to be difficult for Henry. I'm not sure how he'll react. I don't want to upset him. You going over there alone might not be such a good idea."

"I'll pretend I stumbled upon his house."

Mama shook her head. "We need to think about this a little more."

"Mama," I said with conviction. "It seems to me that all of you have done enough thinking. It's time for somebody to take action. I reckon that someone is me."

Mama raised her eyebrows, then smiled. I turned back toward the woods and walked away.

chapter 14

I strode off around the back of the barn, then made my way along the fence line till I came to the path I'd noticed months before. After about fifteen minutes of brisk walking, the path narrowed, surrounded by heavy woods. I began to wonder if I should have taken the ATV. It was farther than I'd realized.

As I walked along, I noticed the flora and fauna in the woods seemed different than ours. Which was ridiculous, I knew. And I couldn't really explain it. It wasn't like I'd walked to another part of the country. I was still right there in our little corner of Georgia. But I felt like I'd been transported to another time and place. My stalwart resolve to go alone to meet my uncle faded like dew beneath the sun.

I heard a pair of sandhill cranes calling to each other as they passed overhead. Their staccato whooping echoed through the trees, turning their familiar chortle into an eerie cry. I lifted my eyes in their general direction, but the meshwork of foliage prevented even a glimpse of the large gray birds.

Despite the oppressive humidity, I hugged my arms across my chest. Out of the corner of my eyes, it seemed as though there was movement all around me. But whenever I turned my head one way or the other, all I saw was silvery-gray Spanish moss dripping from the live oaks growing among sweet gums, cedars, and elm. The long bearded tufts of moss provided shelter for numerous creatures, including spiders, rat snakes, and bats. Each time a faint breeze caught the threadlike masses, they swung gently to and fro, and I could smell the mild fragrance wafting from the tiny clusters of flowers that often went unnoticed.

I rubbed my arms with my hands and shook the creeps from my skin, then pivoted on one heel, trying to get my bearings. I couldn't figure out where the river was from where I stood. Although the path had twisted and curved, at least it was clear and easy to follow. I knew I wouldn't get lost. But I felt disoriented. I looked back the way I'd come. Should I turn around? Go back to get Mama and ask her to come with me? No. I needed to find my uncle.

The path narrowed. I had to duck under low-hanging vines and branches, and push aside the sharp saw-tooth fronds of palmetto scrub, which disturbed countless anole lizards. I couldn't help but chuckle as they scuttled up the trunks of the palm trees and then looked down at me in disdain as they extended their bright orange throat fans.

Then, the light changed ever so slightly. I could just make out a sun-drenched clearing ahead as the dense foliage and dark shadows began to thin. Before I went any farther, I stopped to listen. For what, I don't know. Did my Uncle Henry know I was standing in his woods?

I dismissed my pounding heart as a result of the brisk walk, rather than nerves, then stepped out of the shelter of the scrub. Once my vision was no longer obscured, I stopped dead in my tracks. The claustrophobic unease swiftly changed to one of awe and disbelief.

The path I was following veered off to the left and led directly to a small house set quite far away from where I stood. Its weathered boards were a pleasant gray from age, but the tiny structure was in good repair. It was a typical southern "cracker style," similar to the photographs I'd seen of the home Grandpa Joe had built when he and Grandma Pearl were first married. But what I knew must be Uncle Henry's had more of a quaint character. Maybe because I was seeing it in person. Maybe because it was enveloped in an explosion of confederate jasmine, wild rose vines, and lush wisteria. Each plant was heavily entwined around homemade trellises made of gnarled twigs that were propped against the front of the porch and along both sides of the structure.

Off to the right was the barn. It, too, was weathered from age, but stood solid, without a board out of place. An enormous raised vegetable garden grew between the two buildings—it was at least a quarter-acre and looked meticulously cared for. Other parts of the yard were filled with herb gardens and wild flower beds. There were flowers everywhere.

Mama hadn't told me Uncle Henry was a master gardener.

"Whew," I said aloud in a slow exhale of appreciation of the picturesque scene.

I turned back to face the house. There was no movement from within. And, thus far, no one was opening the front door to offer a greeting. I glanced toward the barn and took a few steps in its direction. The double doors were wide open.

"Hello?" I called out. Nothing.

I poked my head cautiously around the frame of the door and peeked into the barn. I called again, "Hello?" Still no response.

An enclosed lean-to was built off one end of the barn. I looked through the glass pane in the upper section of the door, but the interior was too dark to see anything. I jiggled the black porcelain knob, then decided I shouldn't be opening doors.

Standing in the shade of the lean-to, I turned away from the barn and looked back at the house. What now? I wondered. Some of my hair had come loose from my ponytail and it tickled my cheeks. I pulled the clip from my hair, but before I had gathered the loose tendrils once more, I heard a noise behind me.

I spun around. Just a few feet away, a dog stared at me from the open barn door. He was a mix of some sort and just as cute as could be. His coat was tri-colored, his ears flopped like folded envelopes, and his tail was as brushy as a broom. And that tail was wagging, ever so slightly. He seemed friendly enough. Although it sure was odd that he hadn't barked at my arrival. He just continued to stare at me. His behavior was definitely strange. How many dogs wouldn't at least come up to sniff a stranger?

"Hi there, fella," I said and stepped forward to pat his head. But he immediately backed away. At that very instant, I saw movement from inside the darkened barn and heard what sounded like feet shuffling along the dirt floor.

"What in the world...?" a man's voice exclaimed.

Have you ever noticed how families develop a certain way of talking? And certain phrases become common within that family? Mama said, *What in the world?* So did Daddy. And I'd heard both Grandpa Joe and Grandma Pearl use that phrase, as well.

Now, here was a person I had never even met, but he was someone who was a part of our family nonetheless, saying those same words. I found this very interesting. This might have been a strange thing to think about right at that particular moment, but that's the way my brain works.

"Uncle Henry?" I ventured. I wondered if he could hear the pounding of my heart. "My name is Katherine. Everyone calls me Kip. You can, too. I'm your niece. The one who loves horses. You may have heard of me."

I tended to get chatty when I was nervous.

"I know who you are," the man said in an unfriendly tone I didn't expect. "What in the world are you doing here?"

He remained standing in the shadows of the barn. The only thing I could see were his boots. And his dog, who was now sitting beside him. I started to step inside.

"Stay where you are!" he shouted, startling me. "What are you doing here?"

"We...we're family," I said taking a step back. "I've come to meet you...so...so we can be friends."

"I don't want to be friends. With you or anyone else. And I don't want you here. Ever. Now go home and don't ever come back." I saw him reach down with his left hand and place it on his dog's head.

"I...I need help. With a horse. Did you know I have horses? At...they're at Grandpa's barn. And I have a donkey. I need your help with one of the horses."

"How did you even find me?" he asked, ignoring everything I'd just told him.

"I—"

"It doesn't matter," he interrupted. "Katherine Baker! I want you to leave."

"One of the horses. One of my horses. The black. He has a rope around his neck. I can't get near him to remove it. He's going to get hurt. I need your help."

"Get your daddy to help. He knows as much about horses as I do."

"He won't even come look at them."

"Figures. The stubborn fool."

"Something which seems to be a prominent and problematic trait among the Baker men," I said, startling myself with my sassy tone.

I heard Uncle Henry laugh and thought he was softening to the idea of he and I being friends. Boy, was I wrong. When I reached up and put my hand toward the barn door with the intention of coming closer, before I could comprehend what was happening, he grabbed my arm and moved me backward. The motion brought him forward, into the light. I looked up at his face and dropped my hairclip. The sight of his mangled scars and missing eye made the air leave my lungs, but I did everything within my power not to let my expression reveal how shocked I was. Uncle Henry continued to hold my arm as we stared at each other.

"Are you happy?" he snapped. "Get a good look! 'Cause it'll be your last."

I didn't understand why he was being so hateful. Mama had said he was kind. I'm here to tell you he was *not* being kind. My composure was slipping and I could feel tears stinging my eyes.

"I didn't come here to look at your face," I told him. "I came here to be your friend."

He yanked me closer. "I don't want your friendship," he growled.

"I feel sorry for you," I said through gritted teeth.

"And I don't want your sympathy," he said, still gripping my arm.

"Well, you have it," I shot back. "But it's not because you suffered this injury." I felt tears rising up. "I feel sorry for you because I would be a good friend to you."

That was it for keeping my emotions in check. A sob broke free from my chest. I yanked my arm out of his grasp and turned and ran. When I reached the edge of the woods I stopped and looked back at the barn. Uncle Henry was nowhere to be seen. I stood for a minute, breathing hard, while hurt and angry tears trickled down my face.

I balled my hands into fists and stuck them on my hips.

I huffed out an angry sigh. Then I hollered toward the barn, "My donkey has more sense than you! Do you hear me? He suffered more hurt and pain than you ever did. And he *wants* my friendship. He understands the comfort of having a friend!"

I stomped my foot, just like Liberty Biscuit did when he was mad.

"Do you hear me?" I yelled again. "A little one-eyed donkey with a broken ear and a crooked-y leg has more sense than you, a grown man!"

chapter 15

You said *what?*" Mama asked when I got back home and re-layed what had happened at Uncle Henry's.

"I was so mad," I replied, angry all over again, just thinking about it. "I couldn't help myself."

Mama shook her head, but she was smiling. "Well, all I got to say is, good for you," she said, and then she laughed.

"And the sad thing is, it's the truth!" I was pacing the kitchen. "Liberty suffered years of being abused. He suffered being starved. Did he crawl into a hole and try to hide from the world?" I turned to face Mama. "No! He did not." I resumed pacing. "Is Liberty concerned with his appearance? No! He is not." I stopped again and jutted a finger in the direction of Uncle Henry's. "*That* man needs to literally get a life. And I do mean literally."

Mama raised her eyebrows and pursed her lips. "Mmhmm," she agreed. "That's why I decided to betray his confidence. Enough foolishness from *all* these Baker men."

I sighed, exasperated. "Yep. Enough foolishness!"

Mama then said, "But for now, let's keep this between ourselves. I need to ponder the best approach before we move ahead. Maybe when Grandpa Joe gets home from Savannah, he and I can try to speak to Uncle Henry together."

"You know what else, Mama?"

"Hmm?"

"Uncle Henry is not scary." I thought for just a moment, then added, "Pretty is as pretty does. The ugliest thing about him is the fact that he believes he's unlovable."

Mama just smiled and put her soft hand on my cheek.

The following morning, I found Mama in her office. It wasn't *really* an office. It was what used to be a sunroom off the front hallway. Light flooded the space from floor-to-ceiling windows on two sides. The other two walls were floor-to-ceiling bookshelves. The shelves even went up and around the doorway, then down the other side. Everything was painted a crisp white. Mama's desk was smack-dab in the middle of the room. There were two puffy chairs, upholstered in cheerful yellow and blue flowers, facing her desk. I set my hands on the back of one of those chairs.

"I'm heading over to the barn to check on the horses and spend time with Liberty."

Mama glanced up from her desk. "Okay. Maybe I'll walk over a bit later. I'll bring lunch. We can have a picnic."

"That'd be nice," I said. "Then we can take some crumbs to Flat Rock for my crows."

"Any luck yet? Have they brought you any gifts?"

"I don't view it as luck, Mama. I see it more as benevolence from the universe."

Mama crinkled her forehead. But it wasn't an unhappy look. Her eyes were shining. "Where do you come up with this stuff?" she asked with a smile.

I didn't answer her. Instead, I asked a question back: "Mama? Do you think there are different ways to interpret the word *faith*?"

"Certainly," she said. "Any concept such as that could be interpreted differently by different people. Why are you asking?"

"Remember when we heard the awful news about Miz Prudy?"

"Yes."

Miz Prudy was a beloved member of our community. One Sunday morning, on her own steam, she walked from her home to the church she attended two miles away, just as she did every Sunday morning. When she stepped into the vestibule, she clutched her Bible to her chest, took one gasping breath, and fell face down at the feet of Jesus. Not the real Jesus—that would've made headlines—but a full-length, life-size painting of Jesus.

The faithful who had arrived before Miz Prudy all leapt from their pews and kneeled beside or stood over her, fervently praying till EMS arrived. It grieves me to report that Miz Prudy did not survive. That dear woman. There was some speculation that perhaps if CPR had been administered along with those prayers, there may have been a different outcome. But we would never know.

"Well," I said to Mama. "There's the kind of faith Miz Prudy clung to."

Mama nodded, listening.

"Which," I added, "if you ask me, seems to be somewhat hit or miss and carries a measured degree of risk."

Mama refrained from commenting.

"And then there's a kind of faith...an assurance...that the universe will give us what we look for. There will always be chaos and bad things in the world. But if we look for the good, we'll find it. That's what I mean by a benevolence from the universe." I paused for a moment. "Liberty has taught me that."

"My child, sometimes I forget you're only thirteen."

I promptly reminded Mama I would be fourteen in a few days, then waved goodbye.

Liberty heard the ATV, and, as always, he came running in his awkward little trot to greet me with his trumpeting bray. He stopped with his face a mere two inches from mine and nestled his head on my shoulder. I held him close and kissed his cheek. After we said hello, I went to open the gate so he could hang out in the barnyard with me.

When I turned, something caught my eye. A rope was looped around the top bar of the gate. Attached to that rope was a white hairclip. *My* white hairclip. The very one I'd dropped when Uncle Henry grabbed my arm. Now, here it was. Somehow, it had made the journey from the doorway of Uncle Henry's barn all the way to this gate at the Homestead.

I searched the pasture for the black gelding. He and the bay were dozing under a tree in a far corner. I scrambled through the fence boards and started walking out to them. When

I got closer, I could see there was no longer a rope around the black's neck. I knew there wouldn't be.

I stood there in the pasture, staring at the black horse. I shoved my hands in the front pockets of my jeans and a smile crept across my face as I cast my gaze to the woods and the direction of Uncle Henry's house.

The first thought that crossed my mind was, *I knew telling you my donkey was smarter than you would get your goat.*

And the second thought was, *I am in awe of your horsemanship skills, and I want to learn everything you know.*

chapter 16

I wasn't sure if being good at keeping things inside comes with being an adult, but I'm here to tell you...as a thirteen-almost-fourteen-year-old, it was nearly impossible. In other words, I wasn't any good at keeping my mouth shut. And right now, I had something to say to Uncle Henry.

I put Liberty Biscuit back in the pasture so he wouldn't follow me. I hopped in the ATV and headed down the path to Uncle Henry's house. It got a little tight in a few spots—the fender broke some branches and vines smacked against the roll bar. When I came to the edge of the woods, I pulled the ATV into the clearing of Uncle Henry's yard. I did a quick three-point turn, so I was heading in the direction of *leave,* and then cut the motor and got out.

I stood for a moment looking from the house to the barn. There was no movement around either building, but I felt certain Uncle Henry must have heard the ATV.

I stuck my hands on my hips. "Uncle Henry," I hollered. "It's me. Katherine. Kip. Your niece." I didn't really believe he needed that clarification, it just sorta came out. "You'll recall yesterday? When I said my donkey has more sense than you?" I paused for a moment and once again scanned the house and barn. Nothing. "Well, I meant every word."

I hadn't driven there to tell him that, so I wasn't sure why I did. It was something that just sorta came out. "But I didn't come here to tell you that," I said. I scratched my head.

"Uncle Henry," I hollered again as a way of starting over. "I came here to thank you for getting that rope off my horse's neck. So...thank you! And I also came here to tell you I sure would like to know how you did it."

Suddenly his dog appeared in the doorway of the barn. I offered him a friendly wave, then went back to my speech. "I also came here to tell you," I continued, still yelling, "that there is a very long list of things we have in common. There are many reasons for you and I to be friends. Mostly, 'cause we love horses. Wouldn't that be a nice thing?

Teaching your niece about horses? I believe it would be."

Uncle Henry's dog backed up, retreating into the shadows.

"Humph," I muttered. Clearly Uncle Henry must have called to him. Which also confirmed that Uncle Henry knew I was here and could hear what I was saying.

"Uncle Henry," I shouted as I stomped my foot. "When you figure out a way to be smarter than a donkey, and you want to be friends, I'll be waiting." I stopped to listen. Nothing. "I'm right over there," I said and turned to point in the direction of the Homestead. "Every day. Taking care of my horses and that donkey. Who is. Smarter. Than. *You.*" I felt compelled to punctuate the last few words.

I started to leave, then stopped. "One more thing," I yelled. "I would like to know the name of your dog. He's precious."

I went to the ATV and brought the engine to life. My breathing was slightly ragged. Some of it from shouting. Some of it from feeling emotional. Just as I was about to shift into drive, I thought of something else. I turned the key back to off, then stood up on the seat and peered over the roll bar.

"Uncle Henry?" I shouted. "*One more,* one more thing. Maybe this life you've been given isn't about yourself. Maybe it's about finding ways to give back." I wanted to add, *Put that in your pipe and smoke it,* but decided my little diatribe was beginning to get carried away.

In a calmer tone of voice, and reduced volume, I said out loud, "The word of the day is *benevolence*."

"Antares," said a voice behind me.

To be specific, Uncle Henry's voice. I was lying on my stomach in the yard outside the barn. My arms were crossed above my shoulders, cradling my head. I was watching the geldings and Liberty Biscuit as they peacefully grazed.

I rolled over and sat up. "What?" I said. I tried to appear unfazed over the fact that Uncle Henry was standing in front of me, as though he and I frequently met here at the barn to chat about life and horses. But my heart was pounding in my chest.

He didn't answer me. From where I sat, it looked like he'd forgotten how to talk. At the same time, I felt like I'd forgotten how to breathe.

"What did you say?" I repeated, trying to blink casually.

"You said you wanted to know what my dog's name was," he said, pointing to the little mixed breed sitting sweetly at his feet. "It's Antares."

When he heard his name, the pup looked up at Uncle Henry and panted his approval. Uncle Henry appeared uneasy.

Nervous. He stuffed his hands in the front pocket of his khaki work pants. He kept turning toward the path leading back to his house as though he wanted to be sure it didn't disappear, in case he felt the need to make a hasty retreat.

I decided to shift all my attention to his dog. "Well, hello, Antares," I said. He instantly closed his mouth, cocked his head to the side and stared at me. I got to my knees and patted my legs with both hands. "C'mere, sweet boy." He didn't budge. "C'mon."

Uncle Henry whispered, "Antares." Antares looked up at him, then Uncle Henry tipped his head in my direction. The dog's body language instantly and completely changed. He came bounding over, plopped himself in my lap, and started licking my face.

Laughing, I tipped my face up to the sky to dodge his tongue while I hugged him close.

"Oh, my," I said. "What a sweet boy you are!" I looked over at Uncle Henry. "And so well behaved. I haven't been around many dogs, but that was darn incredible how he waited for you to tell him it was okay to come say hi."

"Not really incredible," said Uncle Henry. "It's simply treating an animal with kindness, and taking the time it takes during training to create a relationship of respect."

"Take the time it takes," I repeated. "You sound like Grandpa Joe."

"Well, he raised me."

"That's a good name," I said getting to my feet. "Antares." We both watched as the pup wandered a few feet away and sniffed along the fence line of the pasture, then marked a post. "A star in the constellation Orion, right?"

"Mmhm," Uncle Henry said with a nod. "How'd you know that?"

"Daddy and I love the nighttime sky. We study the stars. I'm a curious sort. And I read. A lot. When I love something—or someone—I want to learn all I can. The woods, for instance. I love the woods. Consequently, I know more about the flora and fauna around here than a kid my age ought to."

Uncle Henry laughed. I noticed he was keeping his right side turned away from me. Self-conscious of his scars, I figured. This was something I'd have to work on if we were going to be friends. But today wasn't the day. *Take the time it takes.*

"What's so funny?" I asked.

"That wasn't really a laugh, as in 'ha, ha,'" Uncle Henry replied, still chuckling. "It was more a laugh of disbelief. I've never heard a child talk the way you do."

"See what you been missin'?" I said as I pointed a finger at his chest.

He laughed again. This time it was a 'ha, ha' laugh.

"And I'm not such a child anymore. I'm almost fourteen."

"I know. September sixteenth."

"When is your birthday?" I asked.

Uncle Henry set his mouth into a straight line. He shook his head, just slightly, then it became a nod and he said, "Same. Same as yours. September sixteenth."

You might think I'd be pleased to hear this. And I was. But I was also shaken to discover another link he and I shared as family that had been denied because of all this foolishness. I thought maybe Uncle Henry agreed by the look on his face. I decided not to say anything. It wouldn't get back the years we'd lost.

Antares stopped sniffing along the fence and stood up tall with his head in the air. He barked, just once. He was looking at Liberty Biscuit, who was way out in the pasture. My donkey lifted his head at the unfamiliar sound.

"That your donkey with the PhD in human psychology?" Uncle Henry asked.

"The very one," I replied. "But his smarts are probably more deserving of a double masters."

Liberty finally noticed someone besides me was up at the barn, which to him translated into potential treats. Thanks to Mama. He came flailing across the pasture, braying his precious head off.

Uncle Henry looked taken aback. And, in fact, he took a few actual steps back, even though Liberty was safely behind the fence. When my little white tornado came to a skidding stop at the gate, his bray tapered down to a few moaning grunts and Uncle Henry muttered, "Wow." Then, "You know," he added, still looking a bit overwhelmed by the sounds Liberty's beat-up body was able to produce. "I can hear him braying all the way over at my place." Then Uncle Henry looked at me. He was smiling. "That's how I know you're over here. He sounds the alarm."

"Well, come say hi to him."

"How did he lose his eye? Get all these scars?" Uncle Henry asked while he scratched Liberty's neck.

I didn't answer right away. I was watching my uncle and my donkey. Their injuries were almost identical. I swallowed the lump in my throat, then told Uncle Henry all about the man who used to own Liberty and the geldings.

Uncle Henry was, of course, deeply troubled to learn of the abuse they'd suffered. Mine was a family that loved animals. We stood quiet for a moment.

"So, what's this little fella's name?" Uncle Henry asked after a bit.

"Liberty Biscuit," I replied. "'Liberty' 'cause I found him on the Fourth of July. Or he found me, I should say. And 'Biscuit' 'cause that's the first thing I fed him."

Uncle Henry smiled as he continued to scratch Liberty's neck. "Did I see you crying earlier?" he then asked, seemingly right out of the blue. "It looked like you'd been crying when I walked up."

I sighed. "Yes," I said. "You'll discover that, if you hang around with me for any length of time, I cry easy. I'm a cryer." I looked at Uncle Henry to gauge his reaction. He didn't look horrified, so I continued. "I have chosen to accept this about myself and I'm not ashamed. I've reasoned that if it's trying to get out—the crying, I mean—it can't be healthy or sound to try to hold it in. And I am what I am." I ended that little speech with a decisive little stomp of my foot.

"So, what were you crying about? If I may ask?"

"You, sir, are partly to blame."

"Me?"

"Yes, you. Daddy found out Mama told me about you. All that...you being alive stuff." I looked over at Uncle Henry and added, "It seems the reports of your death were greatly exaggerated."

Who would've ever thought I'd get to use that old Mark Twain quote? Not me, that's for sure. Not in a million years. But there it was in all its glory.

Uncle Henry opened his mouth to speak, then looked speechless, and in the end, said nothing.

"Grandpa Joe returned home early," I continued. "Mama told them how I'd trespassed on your land—"

"I'm not sure I'd refer to it as trespassing."

"And that I confronted you and called you dumber than a donkey—"

"Well, that's not exactly what you said."

"And so now they're all up there at the house bickering and snapping at each other about what to do now, and how this should be handled. This should be a happy time. Grandpa's knee doesn't hurt. He's finally back home, and boy, did I miss him. We were planning on spending the day over here at the barn. We were finally gonna name the geldings. But everything's in a tailspin." I paused. "Sorta pretty much because of you."

I'll confess right here and now, I embellished the retelling of what happened when Grandpa Joe returned home. Mama didn't really word things quite that way—for example, I don't believe the word "trespass" was mentioned—but I felt compelled to shake things up a bit. It was time for Uncle Henry to step into his own life.

Uncle Henry stared at me for a minute. Then he looked over at Antares and said, "Antares! Home!" Without an ounce of hesitation, that sweet pup turned and ran toward the path that led to the house hidden away in the woods.

Then Uncle Henry said, "Kip," as he tipped his head toward the ATV, "can you give me a ride up to the house?"

chapter 17

Before we got to the lane home, I slowed the ATV to a stop, then turned off the engine.

"Uncle Henry," I said. "Can I ask you a question?"

"Sure." He stared straight ahead. We could catch a glimpse of the house from where we sat.

"What made you come talk to me?"

"Huh," he sorta half-laughed. "You got a way about you, Kip. It was kinda hard to deny just about everything you said the last few days."

I, too, stared straight ahead. My hands were on the top of steering wheel. I drummed my fingers, thinking. "Why didn't you ever come around for Grandma Pearl?" I asked.

"I did. Somewhat. When everyone was off, busy with the farm and Elise worked in town, I'd come to the house, sit with Mama—your Grandma Pearl. Have lunch. Talk."

"I don't mean come around the house. I mean...come around to living."

Uncle Henry looked off toward the woods. He swallowed hard. I wasn't trying to make him feel bad. And I wondered if I should have just kept my mouth shut. But, as I've said, keeping my mouth shut wasn't something I'd ever be renowned for.

"She never pushed me," Uncle Henry replied. "After the accident, she knew I needed time. And then...my...my desolation became a habit. And Grandma Pearl's tender heart grasped at whatever mercy she could find. It all just became a habit." Uncle Henry was quiet for a moment. "Before you know it, life has passed you by. The years are just gone. Life...is over." He sighed. It was a heavy sound.

I nodded, as though I understood. A slow, sorrowful nod. But I didn't understand why anyone would put off life. Delay living.

I decided we needed a little levity.

"You're not dead yet, ya know. Your life *ain't* over. So...you know. Live."

Uncle Henry slowly turned his head. He stared at me like

I was a train wreck. One of those things you don't want to look at but you can't turn away.

"What?" I asked.

"I'm...I'm trying to comprehend you."

"I'm not difficult to comprehend, Uncle Henry. You just need to get out more. You been talking to canning jars and heads of lettuce too long."

Once again, he opened his mouth to speak, but no words came out.

"Mama tells me you like to read," I said, changing the subject.

"I do," Uncle Henry replied. He seemed grateful for a new topic of conversation.

"That's five," I said.

"Five what?"

"Five things we have in common. Horses...well, all animals, I reckon. Gardening. The woods. A birthday. And reading. Reading makes five."

"Six," Uncle Henry said. "We both love the nighttime sky. That makes six."

"Uncle Henry?"

"Yes, Kip."

"Will you help me work with my horses so they learn to trust? Will you teach me what you know about talking to horses?"

"I will."

"Uncle Henry?"

"Yes, Kip."

"I'd like to give you a hug. That is...if doing so wouldn't put you off."

Uncle Henry didn't answer right away. We had both gone back to staring straight ahead. Finally he said, "I suppose it would not. I suppose."

I turned and put my arms around his shoulders and rested my cheek against his. Uncle Henry put his good arm around me. I felt his chest shudder, and then he was holding his breath. This caused me a bit of concern, and so, wishing for Uncle Henry to start breathing again, I gave him a squeeze and then sat back.

Once again, I looked forward. Uncle Henry, once again, looked in the direction of the woods. I saw him wipe his good eye. We both pretended he wasn't crying.

I stopped the ATV near the back porch. We could hear the muted voices of Grandpa Joe, Mama, and Daddy through the open kitchen window. The sound was calm and peaceful. I wished for a little more spirited dialogue so Uncle Henry wouldn't know right off the bat that I had embellished what was going on up at the house.

I went to the door and looked back at Uncle Henry. Whether the family was bickering or not, I knew this would probably be difficult for him. Especially walking into the Keeping Room for the first time since Grandma Pearl passed away.

He took his time navigating the steps one at a time. It wasn't easy with his bad leg. His heavy boots clomped on the pine boards.

"Kip!" Daddy called through the window from somewhere in the kitchen. "You've been told to leave that donkey at the barn."

I froze. My eyes got wide and I clapped a hand over my mouth. Uncle Henry caught my eye. He put one finger against his lips, telling me not to say anything.

"Who you callin' a donkey?" he demanded as we stepped into the kitchen.

Mama gasped. Then she cried, "Henry!" It was a joyful exclamation.

"Henry?" Daddy looked and sounded confused.

"Henry," Grandpa Joe said, just like he'd say, "It's about time."

Uncle Henry looked happy and sad in equal measure. He said, "Now that we've established who I am, how about we figure out how to be a family again?"

Mama rushed to Henry's side. She hugged him, then took his hand and pulled him farther into the room.

"Come sit down," she said. "Can I get you something to drink? Lemonade?"

Uncle Henry shook his head. "I'm fine, Elise. I don't need anything."

Grandpa Joe went to him and they embraced. "It's good to see you, son," Grandpa said.

"We just saw each other before your surgery, Daddy," Uncle Henry replied.

"I mean here. At the house."

They both smiled. Uncle Henry pointed at Grandpa's knee. "Everything went well?"

"Great," said Grandpa Joe. He lifted his leg and bent his knee a few times by way of a demonstration. "Wish I'd done the surgery a few years ago."

I looked at Daddy. He hadn't said anything, aside from Uncle Henry's name when we first walked in. There was a moment of awkward quiet in the room. We all just stood there.

Finally, Uncle Henry said, "Charlie."

Daddy nodded toward his brother. "Henry."

I rolled my eyes. "Good grief!" I exclaimed with a huff of frustration. "You two do realize you're brothers, don't you? You're the only brothers you're each ever gonna have. And I heard a reliable rumor that you used to be best friends."

"Charlie," Uncle Henry offered. "You've been blessed with a child who is wise beyond her years."

"She's too wise, sometimes," Daddy said.

Uncle Henry paused, then said, "I've been ponderin' some things since Mama died...the Bakers do a lot of ponderin'... and then, Kip sorta barged into my life...in a good way. And, well, she confirmed these things I've been thinking about."

Daddy remained quiet. But he was listening.

Uncle Henry looked around the room. "I'm wondering... would everyone come over to my place? All of you."

"Of course," Mama said.

"Why?" Daddy asked.

"I'd like to show you a few things. And I'd like for us to talk."

Grandpa drove the ATV. Uncle Henry sat up front with him, while Mama, Daddy, and I sat in the back. As we approached the Homestead, Liberty brayed.

"Grandpa, wait!" I called out.

He slowed the ATV to a stop. "What is it, Kip?"

"Could we take a vote on the names I picked out for the horses? Could we name them right now? As a family?"

"That's a wonderful idea, Katherine," Mama said affably. "What are our choices?"

I'd been waiting for this day since the moment the horses were first brought to our farm. Actually, I'd been waiting to name a horse of my own all of my life. I felt as excited as a child on Christmas morning. I scrambled out of the ATV and went to the front so I could see everyone's faces.

"For the bay, I was thinking Fire, in honor of my love of fireflies. And for the black, I was thinking Raven, in honor of my love of corvids." I smiled from ear to ear, and my eyes darted from one member of my family to the other. "Well?" I added.

"Hmm," Mama said thoughtfully. She looked off toward the horses. "I like them."

"Daddy?"

He offered a nod and said, "Those are good names."

"Uncle Henry?"

"Fire and Raven." He gave me a thumbs up.

"Grandpa?" By now I was laughing. I couldn't help it. The horses were a part of our family, and we were *naming* them!

"Excellent names, Kipper!" Grandpa said. "Fire and Raven!"

I clapped my hands and yelled, "Yay!" Everyone else clapped and smiled and laughed, as well. Even Daddy—who didn't really want to be there.

I scrambled back into the ATV and stood on the seat beside Mama, my head poking up through the roll bar. "Fire and Raven," I hollered toward the horses. They didn't look up. I laughed, and hollered again, "Your names are Fire and Raven!"

Grandpa started the ATV and told me to sit down. But he was smiling as he navigated the narrow path through the woods, then parked in front of Uncle Henry's barn. There were at least thirty magnolia trees in full bloom growing in a thick line off each end of the building. Their lower boughs touched the ground.

"Your gardens are gorgeous, Henry," Mama said admiringly. "As always."

"I've got my fall seeds in...several squash varieties. Let me know if you want any starter plants. And I'm gonna try pumpkins again."

Mama walked over to a raised bed full of mums. "I could use some of these mum heads for seed," she said.

"Pinch off all you want," Uncle Henry directed.

"Did you have any of those yellow watermelons that your mama and I planted a few years ago?" Mama asked. "I can't remember if she brought you any."

"Those were the sweetest melons I've ever eaten," Grandpa said wistfully.

"I did not," Uncle Henry said. "I'll have to remember them for next year."

"Are we here to talk about gardens...or what? Why are we here?"

Mama abruptly turned around. She was scowling. "Charles!" she snapped. "What is the matter with you?"

Personally, I was enjoying the garden conversation immensely. It felt like we were a normal family. Whatever that might be.

Daddy lifted both hands in the air like he was about to catch a football. "I've got work to do," he said, shifting his weight from one foot to the other. "The farm doesn't run itself." He crossed his arms over his chest. "I'm really happy for you, Henry, that you have all this free time to garden and plant flowers. That's real nice."

"Charles," Grandpa said.

"While me and Daddy work sun up to sun down," Daddy went on, ignoring Grandpa, "you're over here playing in the dirt."

"Are you done?" Uncle Henry asked.

"Yeah, I am. Now I have to get back to running this farm."

"I didn't bring you over here to see my gardens."

"Then why did you bring me here?"

"C'mon," Uncle Henry said gruffly. He started walking toward the barn. I could see a cheerful red gate in that line of magnolia trees. Uncle Henry opened the gate and motioned for all of us to follow. Grandpa smiled, like he knew what was waiting beyond the trees.

We stepped into a vast pasture dotted with oak trees. Six horses grazed in the field. So this was where Uncle Henry's horses were hiding. It was a beautiful sight.

Daddy shook his head and looked angry. "What is this? Now we get to see that you also play with ponies?"

Uncle Henry whistled. It was a quick, faint whooshing sound. *Fwit.* One of the horses lifted his head. He stared in our direction for a moment, and then began walking over to where we stood. It was a slow amble.

I found it interesting that he was the only horse to respond to that whistle and leave the herd.

As he drew closer I could see there was gray around his muzzle, and he had deep hollows above his eyes. I thought this might mean he was elderly. Something about the horse looked vaguely familiar to me, but I wasn't sure why. I looked over at Grandpa. He was still smiling, in a sad way. I caught his eye. He nodded. But I didn't know what he meant by that nod.

Mama came to stand beside me. She linked her arm through mine. Suddenly, Daddy's mouth slowly opened. His shoulders fell. His entire body looked like a balloon deflating through a pin hole. He turned to look at Grandpa, then his eyes darted to Henry. He looked back at the horse, who was now just a few feet from us.

"Is...is this..." He didn't finish his sentence. He stepped forward and reached for the horse. The horse smelled Daddy's hand, then a soft nicker came from deep down within his throat.

Herr, herr, herr. Herr, herr, herr...

"Is...this Indigo?" My daddy's voice was choked with emotion.

I gasped and put both hands over my mouth. *Of course!* No one spoke. Daddy turned around. His eyes met Uncle Henry's. Uncle Henry nodded.

Daddy turned back to the horse. He put a hand on the old gelding's muzzle. He cupped his hand gently over one of the horse's eyes, closing it—just like I had always done with Liberty. Then he moved his hand to the horse's neck. He leaned forward and put his mouth against Indigo's cheek and took a deep breath. We could hear him whisper something only the horse could hear.

Then, suddenly, Daddy sank down to one knee. He put one hand over his eyes and began to sob.

I started to go to him. Mama grabbed my arm and pulled me back to her side. When I looked over at her, with a confused expression on my face, she only shook her head. When she blinked, tears fell from her eyes.

Grandpa came to stand beside us. There were tears in his eyes, as well. But I couldn't bear to watch my daddy crying. Why didn't someone do something?

Then I remembered what I'd said to Uncle Henry. If it needed to get out of you—the crying, I mean—it wasn't healthy to hold it in. I suspected Daddy had been holding in a whole bunch of crying.

Slowly, Uncle Henry stepped to Daddy's side. He set a hand on Daddy's shoulder. It seemed that Daddy began to cry even harder.

My eyes shifted from Mama to Grandpa Joe and back again. Mama had her hand over her mouth. Grandpa's chin was quivering; he was looking at the ground.

No one said a word while Daddy cried.

Finally, Daddy took a few shuddering breaths. He wiped his eyes on the sleeve of his shirt. Then, without looking up, he reached out for Uncle Henry's hand. Uncle Henry took it, a firm grip like two men shaking hands, and he pulled Daddy to his feet. They stood nearly toe to toe, staring at each other.

Then they both set their mouths in hard straight lines. And then they flung their arms around each other.

chapter 18

"Elise, what would you think about experimenting with a few recipes for peach salsa?"

Uncle Henry and Mama both stood at the sink. Mama was peeling potatoes and Uncle Henry was peeling shrimp. They'd been cooking together nearly every evening since Uncle Henry had come back into our lives. It was like he'd always been here.

"Oh!" Mama glanced over at him. "I love that idea, Henry."

Grandpa Joe was sitting in the nook, reading the paper. I was at the center island, reading a book.

"What idea?" Daddy asked, walking into the Keeping Room, his hair wet from the shower. He was wearing a black tee-shirt and blue jean shorts, but he was barefoot. Daddy's feet never saw the sun. They looked like two belly-up carp, sitting on the hardwood floor.

He walked over to the sink and kissed Mama on the cheek. He clapped Uncle Henry on the shoulder, then left his hand there for an extra moment or two. It felt as though the gesture warmed the entire room.

"Henry and I have been talking about packaging some peach preserves to sell at the farmer's market," Mama said. "We've even looked into getting labels made with the Baker Peach Farm logo and your Mama's slogan. And Henry just suggested branching into salsas."

Daddy looked impressed. "That's a great idea," he said.

"'One Bite and You'll Have a Peach of a Day,'" I said in an exaggerated southern drawl.

Everyone laughed.

Just then we heard a vehicle coming up our driveway. The sound of tires crunched along the gravel, then came to a stop. We couldn't see who it was from the Keeping Room, so I went to the front door.

When I stepped out onto the porch, Jason was getting out of an old Jeep.

"Hello, Kip-Katherine," he called out. His smile made my stomach flutter.

"Hello, Jason Starr with two Rs." I stepped over to the porch railing and wrapped my arms around the post. "What are you doing here?"

"I'm callin' on you," he said. "Is that okay?"

He had on black high-tops, a white t-shirt, and madras shorts with pink as the primary color. I had never in my life seen a boy wearing madras shorts. He made his way to the front steps and put a foot on the bottom one. I couldn't stop staring at him. And it wasn't because I thought he was cute. Although I did. It was because I'd just never met anyone like him. This city boy sure had his own style.

"Are you gonna invite me in?"

"Oh. Sure," I fumbled, stepping back. "C'mon in."

I led Jason into the Keeping Room. When my family saw who was with me, they all stopped talking. I awkwardly made the introductions.

To his credit, when Jason shook hands with Uncle Henry, he didn't react in an unfavorable way. And I watched in particular. It was as though Jason didn't even notice the scars.

"Are you George and Sadie Starr's grandson?" Daddy asked.

"Yes, sir," Jason replied.

"Ah." Daddy nodded approval. "Good folks."

"We heard their grandson had moved here," Grandpa said. "And you plan on going to vet school? Is that right?"

"Yes, sir," Jason said again.

"Well, good for you, son," Grandpa added. "But I imagine vet school isn't easy to get into. You got a tough row to hoe."

"Yes, sir," Jason said. "Because of my age, I'm starting slow. I'm only seventeen. That's why I'm spending a year here with my grandparents. I'll take some preliminary classes and get used to the routine of college before I dive into the full program."

"That sounds like a smart plan," Daddy said.

"Would you like to stay for dinner, Jason?" Mama asked.

"Thank you, ma'am," Jason said. "But no, I can't. I can't stay long this evening." He looked over at me. "Um, I came by...that is, if Miss Katherine agrees..." Then his eyes darted to Daddy. "And if you agree, as well, sir—I was dropping by to introduce myself and ask Katherine to a movie this weekend." He stuffed his hands in his pockets, then took them right back out.

Grandpa coughed.

Was Jason Starr asking me out on a date? I reckoned he was. I pathetically admit right here and now that I didn't know what to do or say. I looked at Mama. Both her eyebrows were raised and her mouth was in the shape of an "O." I looked at Daddy. His eyes were narrowed into slits, and he began rubbing a hand back and forth across the stubble on his chin.

Uncle Henry went back to peeling shrimp. I thought I heard him quietly humming.

Everyone else was quiet. I figured I should say something.

"I would like that," I managed.

"Oh," Mama said, as if surprised. "Well...I think...um, what do we think, Charles?"

"I know Katherine is young, Mr. Baker," Jason said. "But I give you my solemn word that I will behave like a gentleman and have her home directly after the movie ends."

Daddy opened his mouth, then closed it. His eyes shot over to Mama with a look of desperation. Just then we heard Grandpa's paper crinkle loudly.

"You know," he said, "I've been wanting to see that particular show that's playing right now. Why don't we all go?"

"And just what show *is* that, Daddy, that's playing right now?" Uncle Henry asked.

I felt like I was going to start giggling.

"Oh, you know," Grandpa said nonchalantly. "The one with what's his name and who-ya-call-it."

"Oh, yeah," Uncle Henry said without turning away from the sink and his shrimp. "That one. What's it about again?"

"Oh, you know. Some adventure."

Mama rolled her eyes in a comical way. "Alright, you two," she said.

"Actually," Jason said, clearing his throat. "It's a comedy. And it would be just fine with me if you all came along."

Then Daddy cleared *his* throat. "It's not that we don't trust you, son. It's just that, as you said, Kip, er, Katherine is so young."

Mama came over and put her hand on Daddy's arm. "Jason," she began. "Perhaps you'd give us some time to get to know you a little better. Come to dinner one evening? Come enjoy some tea on the porch one afternoon. We can talk. All of us. Maybe you and Katherine could go for a walk around the farm? That sort of thing?"

"Yes, ma'am," Jason said. "That would be just fine." He looked over at me. "That is, if you'd like to spend some time together?"

"I would like that," I repeated, my cheeks warm. I wondered if he could hear my heart skipping like a stone across a smooth pond.

"Could you join us tomorrow for dinner?" Mama asked.

"Yes, ma'am, I could. Thank you." Jason took a few steps back. He was smiling broadly. "For now, I'll let you get back to your evening."

"I...I'll walk out with you," I stammered. I didn't know if I should. I stole a look at Mama. She raised her eyebrows but gave me a sweet smile.

"You have a nice family, Kip-Katherine." We were walking side by side along the driveway. We got to his Jeep and he bumped my side with his hip.

"Thanks." I smiled up at him. "I like 'em okay."

"So," he said, reaching for the door handle.

I realized I didn't want him to leave. "Where'd you get this old Jeep?"

"It's my Grampy's. He's letting me drive it while I'm staying with them. Cool, isn't it?"

I shrugged. "It's okay."

"What?" he exclaimed. "*Okay?* Just...*okay?* Oh, Kip-Katherine. I don't know if we can be friends anymore." He backed away from me dramatically, as though I were a bomb about to go off. I couldn't have stopped myself from laughing even if I'd wanted to.

"I'm kidding," I said as I patted the faded hood of the vehicle. "It's cool."

"Oh, I don't know if I believe you. In fact," he continued, pointing at the house, "you better cancel me coming to dinner tomorrow."

"It's cool!" I hollered through laughter.

Jason gently grabbed my wrist and pulled me forward. "How cool, Kip-Katherine? Just how cool is it?"

"It's the coolest thing on the planet!" I proclaimed. "The coolest!"

"Whew," he said with mock relief, his hand slipping from my wrist to my hand. "That was close. Our friendship may now resume."

I worried my hand was going to get sweaty. I took it from his and stuck my fists on my hips. "Who says I wanna be friends?"

We stared at each other for a moment. Then Jason Starr with two Rs said, "Your eyes say so, Kip-Katherine. I'll see ya tomorrow evening."

After Jason left, I ran upstairs to my bedroom. I looked at my face in the mirror. I can't tell you why. I just wanted to see what my face looked like.

When I came back downstairs, Mama said dinner was almost ready. I told her I needed to go for a walk and suggested they all start without me if I wasn't back by the time they were ready to sit down. It appeared to me that Mama was trying to conceal a smile. But she only nodded, then her eyes found Daddy's.

My mind was in too much of a state to try to figure out whatever silent message they were sending each other.

I ran down the back steps. I ran across the yard, then headed for the red dirt lane that led to Busby Creek. As I neared Flat Rock, I wished I'd brought something for my crows. I drew closer and something on the center of the rock caught my eye.

Whatever it was, it glinted in the gloaming of the setting sun. I took a few cautious steps closer.

My mouth fell open. I felt a shiver run up my spine. Now my mind swirled with wonder and awe.

The crows had brought me a gift at last: a tiny silver chain. It was complete—no missing links, a full circle connected by a clasp. I sat down in a heap next to that chain and just stared at it as I thought about the last year of my life: Losing Grandma Pearl, finding Liberty Biscuit, learning about Uncle Henry and Elizabeth Grace. But mostly, discovering Daddy had struggles and emotions I'd never considered, and realizing that Mama was stronger than I ever imagined.

And I'll admit, along with everything else stomping around in my brain, I couldn't help but let Jason Starr enter my thoughts, as well.

I picked up the chain and closed my hand around it, then held it to my chest. I tipped my head back, searching the tree tops. The echoing call of the crows came back to me.

Caw! Caw!

I looked back down at the chain in my hand and fingered the links, touching them as though they were precious and rare. And really, they were. But not in a way that could change a bank account. More along the lines of my faith in the benevolence of the universe.

I had no food to offer the crows this evening, but I could offer them a poem. It was one of my favorites from an author I liked named Lennon Faris. I loved the poem so much that I had it memorized. I got to my feet and stood in the center of Flat Rock. I closed my eyes, then took several deep and deliberate breaths, filling my lungs with the sweet air from the surrounding woods while my heart filled with a grateful understanding.

Then, I opened my eyes. With a reverence the poem deserved, I squared my shoulders and stood straight and tall and recited the words out loud:

"

Under The Sylvan Sun by Lennon Faris

Two saplings gaze into a pool.

"See my brawny branches," says Oak, stretching.

"And my ample trunk," Sycamore preens,

digging roots into the Earth.

"Your bark's like a fungus."

"Your progeny's the teats of a fox who milked too long."

Why fight? susurrates Wind, joyriding between their leaves.

What do you accomplish?

Ignoring Wind, Oak roars to his squirrel brigade,

"Hurl my progeny at that blasphemous ogre!"

Songbirds of Sycamore dive-bomb

the squirrels, screaming back insults.

War rages in the canopy.

Below, a beaver meanders into the glen.

He builds his home.

Eventually, the silent stumps turn back into dust.

"

I'll tell you why this poem means so much to me and why it has given me so much to ponder.

I'll tell you why I cling to it.

I'm inspired by the way Wind embraces joy despite the folly all around her. *War rages in the canopy.* It's empowering to know the progression of life marches on. *A beaver meanders into the glen. He builds his home.* And the lesson that everything goes full circle, as it should, is a reminder to live. Right now. Today. *The silent stumps turn back into dust.*

I thought about my sweet Liberty Biscuit and how that raggedy little donkey changed my life. All our lives. He taught me that if I accepted certain things about life—truly accepted that the world is a mixture of lavish beauty and withering heartbreak—then I had the strength and the power to create balance.

The broken parts within us could mend when we looked beyond ourselves.

I wanted to be like Wind...

about the author

When Melanie Sue Bowles stumbled across the quote, "The purpose of life is to live a life of purpose," she loved it so much that it became the steadfast philosophy by which she has lived her entire adult life. Unwanted, elderly, and abused horses became her purpose, and she and her husband Jim began Proud Spirit Horse Sanctuary with one horse in need on five acres of land in rural Florida. Their facility grew to hundreds of acres in first Arkansas, and then North Carolina, where rescued animals were allowed to roam as natural herds. Over the years, Melanie and Jim have intervened on behalf of over three-hundred downtrodden horses, many of them coming to the sanctuary to live out their lives in peace and dignity. Their story has been featured on PBS and in three books Bowles has written about the Sanctuary's animal residents. Bowles comes from a large family, many of whom own horses and love all animals as much as she does, including nieces, nephews, and grandchildren who helped inspire the characters in *Liberty Biscuit.*